P9-DCS-277

THE
LAST GIRL
ON EARTH

THE LAST GIRL ON EARTH

alexandra blogier

DELACORTE PRESS

This is a work of fiction. Names, characters, places, and incidents either are the product of the author's imagination or are used fictitiously. Any resemblance to actual persons, living or dead, events, or locales is entirely coincidental.

Text copyright © 2018 by Alloy Entertainment
Jacket design by Mallory Grigg
Galaxy © 2018 Robert Gendler / Schence Photo Library / Getty Images
Sea © 2018 Jens Mayer / EyeEm / Getty Images
Silhouette © 2018 Ostill / Getty Images

All rights reserved. Published in the United States by Delacorte Press, an imprint of Random House Children's Books, a division of Penguin Random House LLC, New York.

Delacorte Press is a registered trademark and the colophon is a trademark of Penguin Random House LLC.

GetUnderlined.com

Educators and librarians, for a variety of teaching tools, visit us at RHTeachersLibrarians.com

Library of Congress Cataloging-in-Publication Data is available upon request.
ISBN 978-0-399-55227-4 (trade) — ISBN 978-0-399-55229-8 (ebook)

The text of this book is set in 11-point ITC Esprit.
Interior design by Liz Dresner

Printed in the United States of America
10 9 8 7 6 5 4 3 2
First Edition

Random House Children's Books supports the First Amendment and celebrates the right to read.

for my mother

one

I push my way through the tangled weeds and onto the cliffs overlooking the Bay. The light of day is already fading, and for a moment, it looks like winter, though there is no such thing. Once there were whales in the waters below, but now there are only skeletons, mammoth in their loss of flesh. I imagine them as they were when they still existed, full of breath and body, before the ocean could no longer hold them.

Vines snake around the buildings below, flowers twisting around the shoots. The whole city pushes out of the land as though it's blooming. Mirabae is already here, stretched out like a starfish, waiting. I stand hidden in the shadows of the trees, but she senses my presence.

"You're late," she calls out, her eyes closed. "I've been here forever."

The gills behind her ears flick open and closed. They allow for the release of air from the body, for breathing underwater. I touch my own gills. They flick open and closed, too, but they let no air out or in. They don't do anything at all.

"Sorry," I say. I don't tell her where I've been.

I drop down next to her, my head to her head, and she weaves our hair together in one long braid. Mirabae's hair is purple and shimmers in the sun. Mine is dark and falls in waves down my back. When we were younger, she would come over at night when her parents fought, scaling up the side of the house to my window, where I always let her in. We would sit on the roof and map out the stars in the sky. There are things I don't tell her, things I don't say out loud to anyone, but I know that when I come to these cliffs, she'll be here, where the world belongs only to us.

"Maybe we should stay here," I say to Mirabae. "Build a tiny home out of twigs. Sharpen our teeth into points."

"Go feral," she says, and smiles. At the end of this week, we start Assessment, the three months of training that will prepare us for enlisting in the Abdolorean Armed Forces. The Abdoloreans call it Conscription. Soon we'll be galaxies away from here and from each other, starting the first of seven years of military service.

"What if we just didn't go?" I ask, as though we have a choice.

"I want to go," she says quietly, staring up at the sky. "I need to get away from here."

"I know," I tell her, and the last train of the day flashes by on the bridge overhead.

Mirabae never talks about her family. Sometimes I wonder if we've been friends for so long because we both have things we hide. I break open a pod from the trees above and crack the seeds from within it. Inside is silver dust, and I pass the pod to Mirabae. We press the powder onto our lips and they glitter. We streak it over our cheekbones so we sparkle in the moonlight.

"We look like jellyfish," I tell her, not that I've ever seen any. The stars shimmer endlessly above, snaking their light over us. My bones twitch relentlessly under my skin. I have no name for what this feeling is. I push myself off the ground, shaking the dirt from my fingers. Mirabae stands up next to me. Nothing more needs to be said. We both know what comes next.

We race down the cliffs, our feet fighting for purchase on the rocky expanse. We weave through fruit groves. We suck on lemons, spitting the seeds into the dirt as we go.

At the base of the cliffs is a tunnel covered in moss. We rush through it, spinning in circles. I don't think about who I am, where I'm going. We don't stop, don't even think of stopping, until we reach the end of the tunnel and find ourselves at the fence at the edge of the beach.

"Let's climb it, Li," Mirabae breathes, her eyes wild. She scales the fence in seconds and looks down at me. "Come on. It's easy."

She pulls herself all the way to the top, balancing on her toes, her dress fluttering in the wind. She spreads her arms wide and leaps through the air as though gravity means nothing. She lands on the other side without even faltering.

"Your turn," she says, smiling.

The fence is twenty feet tall and topped with barbed wire. It's not that high, I know I can climb it, but if anything were to go wrong . . . I can't risk it. Sweat drips down the nape of my neck, the creases of my elbows.

"It's late," I say finally. "I have to go."

Mirabae stares at me through the links of the fence, her smile fading.

"You always leave," she accuses me. "Stay, just this once."

I look up at the moon, full in the sky. I don't know what I can tell her, so I just shake my head.

"Fine," she says, a tinge of sadness in her voice. "Just go."

"Mirabae, you know my dad," I remind her. "You know how he is."

"I know," she sighs, trailing her toes in the sand. "I'll see you tomorrow."

The city sparkles in the distance, a million lights blinking from far away. I walk down street after street, my footsteps echoing on the pavement. Again I look up to the sky and the galaxies within it. "Where am I going?" I whisper. "What does this life hold?" But I know there's only one answer. There's only one way for my life to move.

My house sits on a cliff over a small curve of ocean. All the houses here look the same—three floors of interconnected glass tiers, their frames lined with chrome. Ours is the last one on a long street, set far apart from the other houses.

I go through the backyard, picking a bundle of mint from the plant that snakes along the side of the house. The door opens and shuts automatically behind me, making no sound. I walk into the kitchen. Zo stands by the sink, her back to me, her hair piled on top of her head. She turns around when she hears me come in. Her hair is black, like the ocean on a night when there is no moon. Her eyes are hazel, like our father's.

"Dad's looking for you," she says, a warning in her voice. She's dressed in one of his old shirts, streaked with paint. She pours vials of white powder into different bowls, then fills the bowls with water. The powder bursts into colors as she stirs—blue, purple, green.

"Is he here?" I ask, feeling a twinge of anxiety. I already know what he's going to say.

"He's upstairs," she says. She spreads a canvas across the table, its thin metallic surface rippling as she unrolls it.

"What did you tell him?"

Zo shrugs. "That I had no idea where you were." She dips a brush into the bowl of blue paint.

I fill a glass mug with hot water and drop in the mint. Steam rises into the air and I blow on the water to cool it, waiting for the herb to steep. My father used to bring me a mint infusion at night, placing the mug by my bed. When he first visited Earth, my human parents were the ones who hosted him, teaching him human customs, like how to make tea. He was part of a coalition, one of many scientists who arrived from Abdolora with advanced preservation technology. The damage to Earth was still considered reversible then, the planet not so far gone that changes couldn't be made. No one knew what the future would hold; no one predicted the despair that would follow. Soon after he arrived, the famines came, then the wars—so many humans killed by one another's hands, everyone trying to survive on a dying planet. By the time the Abdolorean council decided that humans weren't fit to survive, my father had taken me in. He hid me in secret on Abdolora until he could return to Earth, one of the thousands sent to repopulate the Bay.

We don't talk about my human parents now. We don't talk about the past. Abdoloreans don't dwell on what's already happened, because there's no way for them to change it. But I'm not Abdolorean. I can't help thinking of my parents sometimes.

My hands clench around the mug, my knuckles pale. The tea scalds my throat as I gulp it down in just a few mouthfuls. I push my chair back and it scrapes sharply across the floor. Zo looks up, startled by the sound, brought back from whatever dream world she goes to when she paints.

I walk up the stairs and into the bathroom. It's dark and growing darker, but I don't turn on the light. I stare at my reflection in the mirror, at the gills my father gave me when I was a baby. They're meant to protect me from discovery. They are my armor, hiding the truth of who I am.

"Li." My father's voice cuts into my thoughts. I take a breath and open the door. My father's hair is dark but his beard is auburn. He's tall and broad; his frame fills the doorway.

"Li," he says again. "Where have you been?"

"Nowhere," I say, curling my hair around my fingers.

"Do you have anything you'd like to tell me?" he asks. I shrug. "Not really."

He presses his hand to the wall. The light turns on.

"How about where you were tonight?"

"I was with Mirabae," I tell him, although I suspect he already knows.

"It's past midnight," he says. "You should have been home hours ago. You know it's not safe for you to be sneaking around in the middle of the night."

"Dad," I say calmly, "I wasn't sneaking around. All I did was hang out with a friend."

He folds his arms across his chest, turning to Zo as she tries to pass by unnoticed.

"You," he says. "You both know the risks. You know what will happen if Li gets caught."

Zo winces, and I know what's running through her head. The Abdoloreans set up a council on Earth called the Agency. Its purpose is to safeguard the freedom and security of all Abdoloreans, to collect and analyze information about the planet. My father told me that humans had similar organizations, but it's not like they did any good. If I'm caught by the Agency, we'll all be killed—me for being human, my family for harboring a planetary enemy.

"You have to watch out for your sister," he tells Zo. She rolls her eyes, but I know she listens to everything our father says. "And you." He turns back to me. "You have to be more careful."

"I'm always careful," I say, tracing the edge of the sink with the tip of my finger. He keeps talking like he hasn't heard me.

"I'm doing everything I can to keep you both safe," he says. "But if you ignore the rules I set, I can't protect either of you."

I open my mouth to speak, meeting Zo's eyes. She shakes her head slightly, her way of saying *No, not tonight. Don't push his limits.*

"What's really going on, Li?" he demands.

"Nothing's going on," I say, and suddenly I'm so tired. I've always known I was different. My father never hid the truth from me. *You're not like Zo or me,* he told me. *There's no one else like you on this planet, in this galaxy, at all.* I knew what that meant, the ways I'd have to hide, the ways all three of us would.

"Can you just leave me alone? Please." My voice shakes and I reach for the door. I see a flash of anger on his face before I close it, but I press the lock pad anyway.

I undress and fill the bath, my hair fanning out around me in the water as I slide in. I look at the stars through the glass of the skylight. Clouds move over the face of the moon and my mind races, my memories stutter. I think back to all the mornings I spent training with my father, lifting weights until my muscles burned, running until my whole body was on fire. I remember the day I realized just how hard I'd have to work to stay alive.

My father woke me before dawn. He took me farther into the forest than I had ever been before, past the cabin, built in secret, where my usual training took place. He led me through the redwood trees, the ground swollen with their roots, gnarled hands holding one another tight, so deep below the earth.

He stopped at the base of a tree, pointing to the top.

"Climb it, Li," he said.

I was eight years old.

The tree rose to the sky, higher than I could see. Still, I knew better than to question him. I unlaced my boots, pressing my feet into the dirt. I ran my hands over the ridges of the bark, lifting myself off the ground. I climbed as high as my body would let me; then my hands slipped. I plummeted, landing so hard, all the air left my lungs. I struggled to breathe, fighting against the pain that spread through me. My father pulled me to my feet.

"Again," he said.

I scaled my way back up. Blood rushed in my ears. My bones clicked. My hands scraped against the bark of the tree, my nails snapping, my palms bleeding. I made it no farther than I had the first time. I fell to the ground.

When I looked up, I saw nothing but shadows. It could have been midnight that far down in the forest. What little light there was moved over my skin like lace. The trees around me had existed here for thousands of years, long before Abdoloreans, before anyone at all. I closed my eyes and imagined pressing myself into them. Shards of bark would pierce the tender space between my ribs, my flesh merging into their hulking frames. My feet would twist into knots. They would grow until they took root, nesting themselves in the dirt.

"I don't want to do this anymore," I told him, keeping my eyes closed. I didn't want to see the look of disappointment on my father's face.

"You have to," he said. "You have to do the work if you're going to fit in."

I opened my eyes, turning onto my side. Next to me was a spray of ferns. I ran my fingers across their feathery leaves, waiting for my father to continue.

"You have to be just as strong and fast and smart as everyone else on this planet. You have to be more than human, Li. You have to be one of us."

He leaned over me, touching my neck, checking my pulse.

"You're ready," he said. "Go."

I squeezed my eyes shut, tears threatening to burst free.

"Go!" he shouted. "Go!"

Comets streak across the sky, bringing me back to

where I am now. I watch their light as they flash through the darkness.

I close my eyes and pull my face beneath the water. I stay there, my body still, my tears blurring with the water; then I scream. I scream until my vision swims and my chest burns and I burst out of the water, gasping for breath.

I know I have no choice. I know this is my life. But this life is a lie.

two

"Zo!" I call up the stairs the next morning. "Zo, come on, we're late!"

"Coming!" she shouts back.

I put on my sandals, lacing them around my ankles, then walk through the kitchen and wait by the door.

"Zo!" I shout again, just as she comes flying around the corner. She races through the kitchen in a flurry of movement. She grabs a plum off the counter, pulls on her sandals, and ties her hair back. She's dressed in a gauzy yellow shirt and loose, shimmering pants.

"Are those mine?" I ask, pointing to the pants as we walk out the door.

"Oh," she says, looking down at her legs like she just realized she had them on. "Can I wear them?"

"You're already wearing them," I say, rolling my eyes.

"So, yes?" she says, wiggling her shoulders up and down.

I smile. "What are you doing?"

"My tiny victory dance," she says, laughing, then takes a bite of plum.

I laugh with her, which feels good after last night. I try to not feel sorry for myself. I try to be strong, but there are times when it's hard. After my bath, I fell into a deep sleep. I dreamed of the other galaxies and flying through the air, weightless and free. Then the sun came up this morning, and with it some relief. Time keeps going. I keep going.

We walk down the twisting roads that cut through the forest, passing a line of houses, their doors opening and closing as kids move through them. School starts earlier for us than work does for most parents. They won't go into the city until the afternoon. I know everyone who passes by, since we've been making this trip together for years.

"Zo!" a voice calls out, and we both turn toward it. Her classmate Devi waves her over, and Zo looks at me and smiles hopefully.

"Go ahead," I say, tugging on one of her curls.

"See you after class," she says as she walks away.

The train station is built along the coastline, high above the ground. A long row of glass chutes extends to the platform overhead. Commuters weave around one another on our way toward them. Disks rise through the chutes in constant rotation, just big enough to hold one of us at a time. I walk up to a chute, stepping through the arched opening and onto a disk. The pressure of my feet on its surface activates its movement, and I surge into the sky. For five seconds, I'm enveloped in total silence; then I'm surrounded by all the chaos the platform holds. I scan the crowd, looking for Mirabae, but I don't see her anywhere. She's always had other friends. I don't mind. It makes it easier to hide all the things I can't tell her.

I walk to the edge of the platform, looking down at the ocean through the tracks below, watching the waves as they crash to the shore. My classmates Suwana and Ranthu rush past, leaping down onto the tracks. They crouch on the rail closest to the platform, balancing on their toes. The train winds around the contours of the coast. It looks like a snake, an eel, coming closer and closer.

"Now!" Ranthu shouts, and they jump back just as the train glides into the station. Everyone spreads out across the platform, gathering in groups of four in front of each compartment. Nava, Sundi, and his boyfriend, Izo, stand behind me. The panel in the center of the compartment slides up and I slip into a seat.

"I'm just saying," Nava says, settling into the seat next to me.

Izo leans his back against the window and stretches his legs into Sundi's lap.

"We know what you're saying," Izo says, already bored.

"I'm just saying," she says louder, as though they didn't hear her. "It is super important."

"We know," Sundi says.

"I mean, this decides everything," she goes on. "Right, Li?"

She turns to face me. Her lips are bright red, her nails painted to match.

"What?" I ask, confused.

"The exam," she says impatiently, like I should already know what she's talking about. "The test basically determines our entire lives."

"Yeah," I say, staring through the windows at the city, my stomach turning. How we do on the exam affects our placement—the better our scores, the higher we'll rank in the Forces. I need to score in the top five percent to be considered for a position as officer.

The test will be hard for everyone, but it will be harder for me. My memory is not as strong as my classmates'. Abdoloreans are capable of absorbing unbelievable amounts of information at a rapid rate. I listen as hard as I can during class, trying to retain everything our magister says, but I still have to study to make up for what I miss. No one can know how hard I work to keep up. No one can know why I go straight home after school. I let people think I'm shy and my dad is strict, and that works, most of the time.

The train pulls into city station and the doors lift. We stream out onto the platform and into the streets, heading toward the amphitheater where our classes are held. Flowers sneak through cracks in the sidewalk, the bright petals of begonias and snapdragons, delphiniums and sweet peas. They hang from doorways, they creep across walls, reminding me that something alive exists beneath the city's unforgiving mass.

The buildings are so tall I have to tip my head back to see where they end. Some are made entirely of glass, others of metallic squares that ripple like waves. They sit close together, sweeping up into the sky. I slip through the spaces between them, walking along narrow pathways until I reach the amphitheater.

The building looms above me, perfectly round and blindingly white. I walk through the doors and through the spiraling hallways, all the way to the top floor. Everyone enters the room in a rush. Usually we're separated into smaller sections, but today all of Level Four is together for our final review before tomorrow's exam.

Mirabae is already inside, slouched in a seat near the back. I sit down beside her. She reaches into the pack by her feet and pulls out two jars of juice, both a murky green.

"For you," she says, holding out a jar to me.

"Thanks, Mir," I say. I take a sip, then spit it back out. "What did you put in this?"

"Grapefruit, spinach, apple," she says excitedly. "And blueberries. And garlic. You don't like it?"

"It's awful," I say apologetically.

She takes a sip.

"Oh, it's terrible!" she cries. "Stop drinking it."

"I'll totally drink your horrible dirt juice," I say, and smile at her. Mirabae can never resist a challenge. She raises her eyebrows in a perfect arch and holds her glass up to mine, clinking the two together.

"I'll finish it if you do," she laughs.

"You're on," I say, and start to chug.

We choke down as much of it as we can, watching each other to see who can drink more. Mirabae is the first to stop, only halfway through the jar.

"I can't drink any more of this," she says, wiping her hand across her mouth. "Stop, Li, it's too gross."

We laugh and settle in our seats as Magister Sethra walks into the room, her crimson robes sweeping the floor. She has a shock of white hair, and her face is lined with deep wrinkles. On anyone else, they would look severe, but she looks dignified. I think about the rings of trees, how they mark years passing, the way they represent a lifetime of wisdom.

"Good morning," she says. "For those of you who aren't in my usual section, I'm Magister Sethra, and I will be conducting your final review today."

The lights dim. Everyone who was talking falls silent, looking up at the screen that spans the room. Magister Sethra begins to speak, quickly and without pausing.

"We will begin today's review by looking at the molecular structure of energy as it pertains to transmutation and oxidation."

Everyone is still, their eyes focused on the formulas that flash by on the screen.

"The process of nuclear reaction requires the presence of an outside particle, while radioactive decay requires no outside particle at all. These are separate and distinct chemical processes, yet the outcome of both is the same: atoms of one element change into the atoms of another element entirely."

We have studied how one chemical transforms into another, how one small shift can create an entire universe. My father's world rearranged the moment he took me in, and that in turn changed Zo's world. When my human parents died, my own world became structured around that loss. There are so many lives that someone could lead, one thing giving way to the next.

I realize that my mind is drifting and look up. A boy is staring at me from across the room. I don't recognize him. He must be from a different section. His hair is so blond it's almost silver. His lips are full. His jaw is strong, his body long and lean. Even from far away, I can see the green of his eyes, unwavering and clear.

He leans back in his seat, keeping his eyes on me. I feel my pulse quicken beneath my skin. A list of chemical compounds appears on the screen, but I barely see them. I look at my legs, smooth the folds in my dress. I look back up. He doesn't blink. I look down at my hands, run my tongue over the sharp ridges of my teeth. The boy shifts in his seat, one knee bent. He leans forward and lifts his fingers so slightly it almost doesn't register as movement. He waves.

"Did you see that?" I whisper to Mirabae.

"See what?" she whispers back.

I look at him again, but he's staring up at the screen. It's as though nothing at all has happened.

"Li," Magister Sethra says, and everyone shifts their attention to me. "Is there something you would like to share?"

Behind me someone laughs under their breath.

"No, Magister," I say, my cheeks flushed. "Sorry for the interruption."

The screen before us fills with maps of all the galaxies, graphs charting out the luminosity of the stars.

"In that case," Sethra says, the corners of her mouth turning up in a slight smile. "You can see here that our system for stellar classification is based on the varying spectral characteristics of the stars."

The rest of review passes slowly, one hour after the next slipping past. I will myself to concentrate on the screen, to focus on what Magister Sethra is saying, but her words blur together. All I can think about is how that boy looked at me. Stopping myself from peeking over at him takes all my concentration.

Finally the screen darkens and the lights turn back on.

"Good luck in your final preparations." Magister Sethra smiles at us. "I will see you tomorrow for your exam."

Mirabae and I walk out of class together, moving through the halls until we're standing outside. We meet Zo in the courtyard, then sit down by the willow trees, waiting for the rest of Mirabae's friends. Cailei, Akia, and Braxon walk across the courtyard. A jolt rushes through me, reaching from my heart down to my fingers—next to Braxon is the boy who was watching me. They stop in front of us, their bodies casting long shadows in the sun.

"Hey!" Mirabae says excitedly, motioning for everyone to sit.

The boy sits down next to me. He turns to face me. His eyes are an even darker green than I thought. They glitter as they catch the light of the sun. Maybe I imagined him looking at me. Maybe it wasn't even real.

"I'm Ryn," he says.

"Li," I say.

"Ryn's new," Akia calls over.

My heart beats against my ribs and I wonder if he can hear it. I look at Mirabae, but she's too busy talking to Cailei to notice anything at all. Cailei's hair is pulled into a bun; the sides of her head are shaved. She sits with her arm wrapped around Mirabae's shoulders, her legs stretched out lazily in front of her.

Braxon settles onto the ground in one fluid motion. He looks older than sixteen, one of those guys who is all muscle and already has a beard. Everything about him is broad—his chest, his shoulders, his hands. He's always bothered me. I try my best to avoid him most of the time.

"Li," Braxon says, his smile predatory. "Where have you been all my life?"

"Ignore him," Akia says, rolling her eyes.

"I will," I say, and everyone laughs.

"We're going swimming," Cailei says.

Ryn is watching me from the corner of his eye. "You should come," he says.

"Li never comes out," Mirabae says with a wave of her hand, doing my work for me. But today I don't want it to be so easy.

"We should get home anyway," Zo interjects, offering me another easy out. But again, I don't take it. I don't know what's happening, but I turn back to Akia.

"Where are you going?" I ask.

"Out to the Cove."

The Cove sits on the farthest point of the Bay, nestled between the cliffs, far away from the city. I've never been there before. I think of what waits for me at home: studying, dinner with Zo, more studying. I could go, I think, watching the light fall over Ryn's face. His lips twitch. He smiles.

"I'm in," I say casually, as though this is something I do all the time.

"You are?" Mirabae and Zo say at almost the same time.

"Yeah, sure," I say, like it's not a big deal. "Let's go. You too, Zo."

Her eyes widen, first with trepidation, then possibility. I'm not the only one who misses out on afternoons at the Cove. We stand up and start to walk away from school. Zo pulls me aside.

"Dad's going to notice we're gone," she whispers, glancing around to make sure no one's listening.

"He's working the night shift," I remind her. "He won't know a thing unless you tell him."

Mirabae turns around, noticing that we've fallen behind.

"Are you two coming or what?" she calls out, her smile wide.

"Yes," I call back, staring at Zo. "We're coming."

Zo says nothing to contradict me.

"Finally!" Mirabae says.

Finally, I think, and fall into step with everyone else.

three

We walk until the city is far behind us, turning down the narrow paths that lead into the forest. Mirabae, Akia, and Cailei swing from the branches of the trees. I'm dismayed to see Zo walking with Braxon, her laugh carrying through the air. To distract myself, I pick flowers as I go, weaving them together, stringing them around my neck.

"So," Ryn says, walking up beside me. "Mirabae said you don't come out much."

"Not really," I admit, and I feel my stomach drop.

The leaves sway on the trees overhead. He reaches his arms up, trailing his fingers over the branches hanging over us. "Why not?"

"My dad is kind of overprotective," I tell him, the excuse I always use. "He's strict about us going out."

Ryn's quiet, and I realize that he's waiting for me to say more.

"It's how he's always been," I add. "He's raising me and Zo by himself, so I think he worries we'll get into trouble."

Ryn glances at me. "What happened to your mom?"

"She and my dad were some of the first inhabitants of Earth. She contracted radiation poisoning and died right after my sister was born."

This is the story I've been trained to tell. It's the story of Zo's mother, and though I don't remember her, I know she took me in and raised me as her own daughter. She got sick weeks after Zo was born. During the Abdoloreans' first few years on Earth, emissions levels in the atmosphere were uncontrollably high. Radiation poisoning was a common death, before Abdolorean scientists developed geoengineering techniques to reverse the atmospheric damage. Those who died are thought of as brave pioneers of a new world. Their loss was for the greater good. It's barely even registered. They existed, then they didn't, and everyone moved on with their lives.

"What do you do, staying home all the time?" Ryn asks.

"Mostly just stare at the wall," I say wryly. He laughs. The wind whirls past and I feel the way the forest moves.

We walk through the woods, passing by the quarry,

an empty basin long abandoned. The machines used for mining have rusted over, their wheels flat, their yellow paint flaking. They look like monsters left to lurk behind the trees, their claws stretched out like reaching arms.

"Actually, I read a lot," I amend, looking down into the deep yawn of the quarry as we circle around it. "My dad's a scientist in the Interplanetary Research and Development Program, so he has a lot of good books, mostly on the outlying galaxies and planetary systems."

"Cool," Ryn says, like he really means it.

We reach the edge of the forest, coming up on the Cove. The trees grow thinner around us. The dirt gives way to grass; the grass gives way to sand. We walk between the curves of rocks, looking out at the ocean. I feel something loosen in my chest as I slip onto the shore. Ryn turns to face me, so close I could touch him.

"Let's swim, Li," he says, walking to the shoreline.

I walk behind him, stepping into the footprints he makes in the sand. I study the jut of his shoulders, the curve of the back of his neck. He dives under the waves, but I stay back on the shore. He swims past the edge of the cliffs, past everyone else in the water. He is farther and farther away from me. I couldn't reach him now, even if I wanted to.

Zo comes up next to me and we stand at the edge of the water. We let the ocean lap over our feet. "Look at this place," she says, taking it all in.

The ocean is the deepest blue, the sand as white as bone. I see kids I know from class shouting and laughing and diving off the long line of rocks far out in the water. Nava stands on Sundi's shoulders. Ranthu and Izo run through the sand. Cliffs rise high above the water, curving around the shore, the waves crashing wildly up against them.

Mirabae races across the shore, laughing as she goes. She dives into the water in her bra and shorts, waves rushing over her body. Tiny bubbles rise to the surface as her gills flicker. She's underwater for a minute, then more; then she surges into the air.

Zo slips her dress over her head. As she does, I see the flash of her tattoo, a crescent moon, high up on the inside of her arm. I have the same one, only mine is hidden low on my hip, where no one can see it but me. She heads into the water, her black hair floating behind her.

I keep my clothes on and follow her out. The water rises to my knees, my chest, my shoulders. I plunge beneath the waves and open my eyes. It takes a moment for everything to come into focus. Once it does, I see the slow sway of everyone's limbs in the water, their bodies moving to keep them afloat. I stay underwater for as long as I can, then come up to the surface, careful to keep my breathing even.

Mirabae is right—the water feels amazing. It's peaceful, so unlike the swimming my father made me do when I was younger. He attached weights around my arms and legs to keep me underwater. He held me down when I struggled, his hands pushing on my shoulders as I thrashed. *I'll never let you drown,* he would say after I came up gasping, but there were times when it seemed like he would. All his training was worth it, if only for moments like this. I glide up next to Mirabae, my body moving smoothly through the water.

"That boy is watching you," she says once I reach her, her voice lilting. "Ryn."

I can't stop myself. I turn around and look. He's out by the line of rocks in the distance, talking to some girls I don't know, but his eyes are on me. I resist the urge to dive underwater and hide.

"Hey," Mirabae says, watching the clouds move across the sky. "What do you think of Cailei?"

We tread water, our arms and legs moving in slow circles.

"I don't know anything about her," I say. "But she seems nice."

Mirabae smiles. "I think she's into me."

I look down at my feet, my toes long and distorted in the water. "Yeah? Are you into her?"

"I'm not sure yet," she says. "She kissed me the other day, when we were all out at a party."

She says this like it's no big deal, like she's always out at parties being kissed by girls.

I squint up at the sun. "You went to a party the other day?"

"Yeah, Ranthu had some people over," she says. I don't feel jealous, or even left out, but for a moment I wonder what it must be like to live her life, or anyone else's but mine. I've always known that I can't have the same things as other people my age—boyfriends, normal friendships. Letting myself want them would only make me miserable, so I convince myself that I don't want them at all.

"So what happened?" I ask. "After she kissed you."

"Nothing, really." Mirabae shrugs. She flips onto her back, bringing her arms above her head, clasping her fingers together. "I could be into her. She's smart and funny and she's super hot."

We swim back to shore and stretch out in the sand. Zo lies beside me. Braxon is perched high above us in the branches of a tree. Cailei and Akia sit together, imagining all the different planets where they might be placed for service.

"What about Pesna?" Akia asks. "Everyone says it's a beautiful planet."

"Too cold," says Cailei. "Too many mountains."

"Narin?"

"I could do Narin." Cailei nods. "You know everyone there is really tall, like twice our height? It's crazy."

Ryn steps out of the ocean, onto the sand, his skin glistening with beads of water. Mirabae nudges me, watching me watch him.

"Hey!" she calls out. "Ryn! Come talk to Li!"

"Mir, stop!" I hiss. "We barely know him."

"This is how you *get* to know him," she says with a laugh.

He comes over and sits down next to me. He runs his hands through his hair, shaking the water out. I trail my fingers in the sand slowly, trying to think of something to say.

Before I can start a conversation, Braxon leaps down to the ground, landing in front of us.

"So," Braxon says, towering over me. "I heard you're gunning for officer."

I look over at Zo. She looks down guiltily, avoiding my eyes. I shrug.

"Me too," Braxon goes on, looking me over. He has the kind of arrogance that comes from being the best at everything and knowing it. "Good luck."

"You too," I say shortly. I don't want to get caught up in any more competition than I have to, especially with someone like Braxon, who thrives on it.

He flashes me a tight, unreadable smile, then turns to

look at the group. He points to the cliffs above. "I dare you all to jump!"

"You're on!" Cailei shouts back. She and Akia race toward the cliffs, kicking up sand as they go.

"What about you, Li?" Braxon asks, a challenge in his eyes. "Think you can handle it?"

My heart beats in my chest, pressing up against my lungs. The cliffs rise a hundred feet in the air, higher than I've ever climbed before, farther than I've ever jumped. They curve around the water's edge, jagged and steep. A climb like this is nothing to everyone here. To me it could be deadly. I feel my pulse speed up, the blood rushing through my veins. I have no good excuse, no valid reason to say no.

"Li can handle anything," Mirabae says.

Braxon laughs. "I bet she can," he says. He turns and walks to the cliffs, stretching his arms up to the sky.

Zo looks at me with a flicker of fear in her eyes. *We shouldn't have come here,* her look says. *This was a mistake.* We both know how high that jump is, but if I leave now, it will only be suspicious.

"I'm in," Mirabae says, standing up and slipping her top back on. She looks at me and winks. "Come on, Zo. Let's do this."

Before Zo can say anything, Mirabae grabs her hand, pulling her toward the cliffs, leaving me alone with Ryn.

I stare out at the water, up at the sky, looking anywhere but at him. He leans in closer to me.

"I'll jump if you do," he says. I look up at the cliffs; I look at the way his lips curve when he smiles.

"Okay," I say, not sure what else to do. We stand up and head to the cliffs, his hand brushing mine, just once, as we walk.

We line up alongside everyone else. I press my hands against the cliff, searching for cracks in the stone. I can do this, I remind myself. I've trained my whole life to do what's practically impossible. Braxon crouches in the sand, then leaps up and grabs hold of the cliff. Cailei, Akia, and Mirabae follow. Ryn reaches up and lifts himself off the ground, climbing quickly, easily. Zo swings herself up, glancing down. She looks scared to see me behind her, but she can't say anything without the others hearing her. I force myself to smile at her, to hide the panic rising in my chest. She turns without a word, climbing effortlessly, as though her body weighs nothing at all. I raise one arm, then the other, scaling across fault lines, moving higher and higher away from the ground.

The cliff stretches out endlessly around me. Water drips down fissure lines. All I see is stone. I feel the rush of adrenaline, the exhilaration of height, every muscle in my body moving at once. Everyone else is far above me, their strength boundless compared to mine. I wish I'd gone straight home, the way I always do. I don't know what I was thinking coming here at all.

I reach up, stretching my arm as far as it can go. My hand slips. My legs swing out from under me. I hang off the side of the cliff one-handed. There's nothing to keep me from plummeting. I picture myself splayed on the rocks below, bloodied and lifeless. A shiver of fear runs through me.

Keep going, I think. *Just keep going.*

I grab hold of the cliff with my other hand, pulling my legs back up underneath me. The bottoms of my feet scrape against the stone. Zo and Mirabae are already at the top. I watch them jump, flying through the air, their bodies arched toward the water. My legs shake, my lungs burn, but I can see the top of the cliff. I'm so close to reaching it. I finally grab hold of the ledge, swinging my legs up over it.

Stones break loose under my feet. They skitter down the side of the cliff, disappearing into the air. I look down at the ocean, so far below. Behind me, Akia shouts. Cailei throws her over her shoulders and runs toward the ledge, leaping off the cliff. Akia flips away from her in midair. They slice through the water with barely a splash. They look like minnows, their bodies tiny and dark.

"You scared?" Braxon asks, and I turn around to face

him. I doubt he knows what fear even feels like. Ryn watches me, his face quiet, unreadable.

"Nothing to be scared of," I lie.

Braxon walks to the edge of the cliff, lifting himself up onto his toes. He flips off, sailing backward through the air, spinning in circles, slipping under the waves. Ryn comes up next to me and we are the only ones left. There's no way out of this now.

The ocean stretches out for miles around us. Coral reef decays in the water below, a sprawling graveyard across the sand. Rocks jut up from the shore. My breath catches in my throat. My heart pounds so fiercely it could break me. There's only one thing for me to do.

"Ready?" Ryn asks. I close my eyes. I bend my knees.

"One," he says.

I press my toes against the earth.

"Two."

He slips his hand into mine.

"Three."

We jump.

Everything blurs together as we fall—the gray cliff, the green leaves, the gleam of light off the ocean. The world around us is vibrant, breathing. I spread my arms like wings, and then I'm flying through the air. I forget where I am; I forget everything except this feeling. Then the curve of the ocean rises up to meet me.

Water shatters around me like glass. The current shifts, dragging me under the waves. I spiral through the water, my body spinning until I don't know which way is up. I thrash my arms and legs, but I can't break free from the waves crashing over me.

The weight of the ocean presses down on me, a thousand pounds of pressure. The sky shimmers, but I'm too far down to reach its light. This is what all my training was for, but I can't summon it now. I sink to the ocean floor, the sand rising around me. I'm breaking open, I'm splitting apart, I can't hold my breath any longer. Water rushes into my lungs. My mind goes blank. The world goes dark.

four

Beams of light break through the water. The sky wavers above me, so far away, and I raise my arms as though I can reach it, as though I can save myself.

Fight, Li, my father's voice echoes in my head.

I almost died once, when I was nine. It was late. I was standing on the wires tied between the trees behind our house. My father had strung them there, woven like a spiderweb, a maze for me to work my way through.

It was beautiful in the forest that night, magical even. Mist hung in the air. Moss covered the ground. The line swayed with the weight of my body. I was high above the earth, small against the vast expanse of the sky. My father stood below me, urging me to go higher.

My hands reached for the wires. I swung myself around, twisting in and out. I leaped forward and let go of the wire I was holding and landed on the one below. Then my feet slipped out from under me. My neck snapped back. I fell, flying through the air. My skull cracked against the ground. I tasted the blood as it dripped down to my mouth, then I drifted under, far away from it all.

I woke up with a concussion, my ribs sore, my head pounding. My father later told me he was certain I was going to die. That fear never left me—my life is so fragile, my body something that could betray me so easily.

Now I close my eyes. I let the ocean take me. All at once, I feel the press of arms around me, pulling me up through the waves. I surge above the water, gasping; then I hear Ryn's voice.

"Breathe," he says quietly. "Everything's okay."

It all flashes back to me—our jump off the cliff, our dive into the water, the way the ocean devoured me whole. Panic floods me, bitter in my mouth.

My mind races, my thoughts confused. Of course my gills didn't work. He just saved me from drowning. *He knows,* I think. *He knows.* I pull in breath after breath, trying to slow the rush of blood in my veins.

"Ryn," I whisper. He holds me close, his skin against my skin. I press my head against his chest, feeling the steady pulse of his heart. He tucks my hair back, his fingers brushing against my neck, and it's then that I realize what I'm doing, just how close to him I am. I twist away from him, slipping out of his arms, and swim back toward the shore.

"Li! Wait!" Ryn shouts, but I keep swimming, my arms slicing sharply through the water. I can barely think, barely breathe, but I don't stop until I've reached the shore. I step out of the water and onto the sand, my body swaying slightly. I close my eyes to steady myself. Desperation swells inside me. My eyes fill with tears, but I don't let them fall. I can't lose control, not now, when there are so many people around. I look into the distance, willing myself to hold it together.

Zo stands on the shore, talking to Braxon. He leans close to her and says something I'm too far away to hear. She tips her head back and laughs. She puts her hand on his arm, her eyes shining. I take one shaky step after another until I'm standing beside them.

"Zo," I say, "let's go."

She turns to me and her face lights up. "Hey. You made it."

I wrap my fingers around her wrist and pull. "We're leaving. Now." The smile on her face quickly disappears. She bites her lip, then turns to Braxon.

"I guess we're out of here," she says lightly. "See you around."

Zo and I head toward the trees. I look back to the water, watching for Ryn. In the low light of the setting sun, his features look sharp, almost lupine. I watch as he dives under the waves, vanishing before me, like he was never even here at all.

Zo and I go back through the depths of the forest, the sun setting quickly now, the sky growing darker with each step we take. Zo walks along the length of a fallen tree, her arms spread out for balance.

"I saw you, you know," she says quietly. "I was waiting for you to jump before I swam to shore. When I saw you and Ryn surface, only then did I start talking to Braxon." She grins at me. "He's really cute."

"Zo, I need to tell you something," I say, my voice shaking.

"I'm so happy that we came here today," she says, as though she hasn't heard me. "For once we got to do something normal. And—surprise!—we survived." She looks down at me from her perch on the log. "What were you going to say?"

"I'm going to tell you something," I say carefully. "And I need you to not get upset."

She's silent, watching me, waiting for me to say more.

"Something happened back there," I say. "When I

jumped into the water, I hit some kind of whirlpool, and I got trapped underwater. I almost drowned, and Ryn, he saved me."

"Li!" Zo gasps. All the color leaves her face. "Saved you how?"

"It felt like I blacked out, and when I woke up, Ryn was pulling me to the surface." Just saying the words out loud is enough to make my lungs feel like they're filling up with water, like I'm back beneath the waves. "He told me to keep breathing and that everything was going to be okay."

"You felt like you blacked out or you did black out?" Zo asks sharply.

"I don't know," I lie, my voice breaking. Either way, it doesn't matter. Anything coming close to losing consciousness is abnormal.

"It's not as bad as it sounds," I try, but Zo shakes her head fiercely, interrupting me before I can say anything more.

"This is serious, Li," she insists. "What if you'd gotten hurt?" Earth used to have doctors to take care of people when they got sick. But the Abdoloreans don't get sick. They don't hurt themselves. If I got hurt, there would be no one to go to. No one to examine my body, no one to heal me.

"Zo, please," I say, trying to keep the desperation out of my voice. "It's not that big of a deal."

"We can't keep something like this a secret," Zo whispers, her eyes darting around the forest. "You have fake gills, Li. And now Ryn knows it!"

"Zo!" I cry out. "Really, it's fine. I'm fine. Ryn doesn't know anything. He didn't act weird at all." I let out a clipped laugh. "What's he going to think, anyway? That I'm *human*?"

She stares at me as though she's trying to see through me. *Nothing even happened,* I repeat in my head, over and over, as though thinking it can make it true.

"If you tell Dad, you'll get in just as much trouble as me," I warn her. "You know how angry he'll be. At both of us." I shrug. "And what's the point? I'm okay."

Her eyes flash with hesitation. Our father will blame me for being careless, but he'll blame Zo for letting me go.

"You know I'm right," I say, and her shoulders sink, resigned.

"Fine," she says tightly. "We won't say anything. But you have to promise you won't do something so stupid again. And if Ryn even suspects . . ." But we both know there's no point in finishing that sentence.

The sun sinks below the horizon. The first stars of the night appear in the sky. We move through the trees, neither one of us talking. Soon we reach the city, walking quickly to the station. We ride the train in silence. I avoid Zo's eyes, looking out the window at the world around us. The city lights fade behind us as we move over the tracks. It's not until we're off the train, walking through the streets to our house, that the pressure in my chest fades and I feel myself breathe evenly.

"What did it feel like?" Zo asks quietly. The moon slips behind the clouds.

"What did what feel like?" I ask.

"To drown," she says.

Zo has always been curious about my humanness. What it felt like to twist my ankle or cut my finger peeling fruit or get a bloody nose. There are so many differences between our bodies. I try to find the words to explain my fallibility in a way she can understand.

"Like I was stuck under a landslide," I say. "It felt like I was being buried alive."

The moon reappears, bathing us in light. We emerge from the trees, the sky sparkling above. We turn down street after street, keeping to the shadows until we reach our house. The windows are dark, the whole house still. We walk around the curve of the cliff. Zo reaches for the door, about to open it, then stops, her hand hovering in midair.

"You're sure, Li," she says, staring at me hard. "You're sure Ryn doesn't . . . I don't know. Suspect anything?"

I look up, my eyes tracing the shapes of the constellations until I find the one I'm searching for—the girl filled with stars, alone in the sky.

"Li?" Zo says again, and I turn to her. I think of Ryn's arms around me, his eyes in the light.

"I'm sure," I say, lifting my hand to the door, and my voice sounds steady and clear.

I move around the kitchen, getting dinner ready. I cook squash and peppers, carrots and eggplant, searing them quickly on the electric blue light of the stove. Zo and I eat in our own settled silence. We have our own rhythm, one that can only be found by sharing a life. Zo clears the table, humming as she washes the dishes. She's a year younger than me, but she's already as tall as I am, something I'm not sure I'll ever get used to. After she's done cleaning up, she sits back down at the table, her chin in her hand, and studies my face.

"Let me sketch you," she says impulsively. "The light on you is amazing right now."

"No way," I say. My mind is still buzzing from the jump. All I can think about is Ryn and what he might know.

"Come on," she presses. "How else am I going to remember what you look like after you leave?"

She's joking, but her voice is tinged with sadness, so slight I might miss it if I didn't know her so very well.

I relent, turning toward her in my seat.

"Tilt your head," she says, opening her sketchbook, the paper inside silver. "Stay still."

"I am," I say, fidgeting with my hands.

"No, you're not," she scolds. "Stay really still."

She pulls a pen from her hair. Her eyes flit over my face. Her hand moves across the paper in long, even strokes.

"Done," she says after a few minutes, holding the paper out to me. "Here, look."

She's captured everything—the dark curve of my eyebrows, the freckles high on my cheekbones, the slight crookedness of my nose from when I broke it during training so many years ago.

The false gills on my neck.

"You're really good," I tell her, and I know by the smile on her lips I've made her happy. I look at her, studying her face as she studied mine. She looks so much like our father it startles me. They have the same willowy fingers, the same shadows underneath their eyes. I know that it's not easy for her, being my sister. She lives her life in hiding, too.

"Thanks," she says, tucking the drawing back inside the sketchbook. "I need to practice more, but . . ."

"It's late," I say. "You should get to bed."

"What about you?" she asks. "You should sleep before the exam."

"I'll be up soon." I don't tell her that I have to study all night. It will only make her worry.

"Okay." She yawns. "See you tomorrow."

I wait until I know she's asleep, then go into my father's study. The walls are covered in framed displays of butterfly wings and beetles, creatures my father studied while trying to find a way to protect the more fragile lives from extinction. The shelves are lined with tangles of seaweed, jagged-edged mussels, the lonely shells and spindly legs of horseshoe crabs. They're nothing more than empty husks, but they once pulsed with primordial life, reminding me of a world I was never a part of. I reach past them to the thin-spined books, pulling down the ones I'll need for the night. I open a book on ecological conservation. The screen glows in the darkness. I scan one page after another, the whole way through. I start in on another book, and then another after that.

By the time I look up, it's almost dawn. My eyelids are heavy. Soon the sun will rise. I want to lay my head on the desk and fall asleep, but I have so much more material to study. I read the same sentence over and over, its meaning lost on me. I'm buried so deep within the words that I don't hear my father slip through the door.

"Hey," he says. "What are you doing up?"

I tell him the truth, at least in part. "Review was really hard. I needed to study more."

He sits down beside me and pulls the book toward him.

"Okay," he says. "Let's see what we have here."

He bites his lip as he reads, just as I do, and I am reminded suddenly and fiercely that I, too, am his daughter. I, too, share my life with him.

"I'm sorry about yesterday. I shouldn't be so hard on you." He gives me a small smile, and a wave of guilt washes over me. I shouldn't have gone to the cliffs. I put us all at risk.

"Now, this isn't too difficult," he goes on, turning back to the screen of the book. "Stellar nucleosynthesis is just transmutation. It occurs when the natural abundance of elements within stars varies."

He outlines all the elements in the universe, going over all the different versions of those elements a star can have.

"What's next?" he asks.

I open another book, scanning through the first page, my heart sinking in my chest.

"The chemistry of the bomb," I say.

We go over the formulas. It's there in the math—we find the same truth every time. The bomb was designed to kill all humans on Earth, and it almost did just that.

"Do you get it now?" he asks.

"Yes," I say, then pause. My brain is finding it hard

to process all this information without sleep. But it wouldn't matter how many nights I'd slept for, this is something that will never make sense to me. "No. No, I don't get it."

"Let's go over it one more time," he says, scanning the book back to the beginning.

"I get how the equations work," I say, lacing my fingers together tightly. "I just don't get why everything happened this way. I don't get why there was a bomb at all."

My father sits back in his chair. Silence hangs heavily between us.

"Neither do I, Li," he says softly. "That's why I saved you."

"But I'm the only one you saved," I say.

He looks off into the distance, as though he's remembering everything that happened when he first came here.

"I did everything I could," he says. "I wasn't able save everyone, but believe me, I tried."

"What do you mean?"

Day has begun to break, filling the windows with light.

"I believed in saving the human race," he says slowly. "I believed in integration. I begged the Agency to implement it, but they considered humans unworthy of life on this planet. Humans had inhabited Earth for thousands of years and brought it to the brink of disaster. They'd had so many chances. The Agency didn't think they deserved another. Then, after the bombing, there was only so much I could do."

There were humans who lived through the bombing, somehow surviving the attack. Their bodies were ravaged, the radiation seeping quickly into their bones, but for a matter of weeks, they were still breathing, still alive. Their corpses were found deep in the forest, already turning to ash. Only one woman survived longer, making it all the way to the border of the Bay before she was caught. She was placed in a medical facility, where scientists studied her genetic code and harvested her blood to develop immunizations for earthborn diseases. She was a living experiment, proof that there are some things in this world worse than death.

In the images they show us at school, her eyes are closed. Her bones poke through her pallid skin. Tubes run the length of her arms, and her blood is collected in glass vials. Her head is shaved, her neck revealed. The skin behind her ears is unmarked, smooth. Her name is written at the end of the bed she's bound to: *Ava.*

The first time I saw her, I was young. I remember my heart clenching, like someone had reached into my chest and wrapped their fingers around it. I remember thinking that this could have happened to me if my father hadn't saved me, hadn't taken me off the planet before the bomb exploded. I searched those images for some semblance of familiarity, a way to recognize myself in Ava's body, and found none. Eventually she died, too, captured and alone.

I listen to the pull of the waves on the shore, the strange hiss of the wind through the stalks of seagrass. I've never heard my father talk about the past like this before.

"Thank you for trying," I say, my voice small.

We stare out the window at the sunrise. Neither of us says anything more. We sit like this for a long time, the quiet of dawn settling around us.

"You should sleep," he says finally.

"Yeah," I say, but I know that I won't. I rest my head in my hands. There are only a few hours until the exam, until my future is mapped out in front of me.

"Li," my father says, and I raise my eyes to his. "No matter what anyone says, I want you to know that you always have a choice. You can choose to do the right thing." He pauses. "Sometimes doing the right thing isn't doing what you're told."

He stands and walks to the door, talking to me over his shoulder.

"If I had done as I was told, you wouldn't be here with me." He hesitates, as if he's not sure what he should say.

"I've always worried about how you're going to survive. But I'm beginning to see that you have to do more than survive. You have to live."

With that, he closes the door behind him, leaving me alone to think about what he really means.

five

"Hi! Wait up!" Mirabae calls as I navigate the hallway at school. She slips through the crowd and comes up beside me.

"Hey," she says. She's wearing a low-cut shirt and very short shorts. Her hair is in loose braids. I know she's reveling in dressing how she wants to. Once we're in the Forces we'll be wearing the regulation uniform.

"Hey," I say back. "You ready?"

"Of course. Why wouldn't I be?"

I shrug.

"I'm not too worried about it," she says. "It's just our history and legacy and everything else we've been taught over and over for the past eight years."

I laugh, and for a moment I forget how nervous I am.

She studies me, raising an eyebrow. "You look a little rough."

"Yeah." I'm wearing pants that rest low on my hips and an old, worn shirt that I borrowed from Zo. I reach up to my hair and try to work through the tangles. "I didn't really sleep last night."

"Too busy thinking about kissing Ryn?" she teases, an excited glint in her eye. "Tell me everything."

"I have no idea what you're talking about, Mir," I say, making my way into the amphitheater.

"I saw you with him in the water, Li. You looked like you were getting along well." Her lips curl into a smile. "Don't leave anything out. I want every last detail."

"I don't know. . . . We didn't really talk."

She laughs. "Oh, I like the sound of this."

"It's not like that," I say, heat rising to my cheeks as I remember the feeling of his body against mine. I wish I could tell her what actually happened, how I almost drowned, how worried I am that Ryn knows there's something different about me. A new current of fear runs through me now.

Mirabae rolls her eyes as she takes a seat, and all of a sudden we remember what's coming next. "Good luck, Li," she tells me, squeezing my hand.

"You too, Mir," I say, and slip into an empty row

near the front. Above each seat is a hologram, situated as though it's a desk. I lower my hand over it, its surface smooth against my skin, like I'm pressing my palm against water.

Welcome, Li. The hologram glows.

I close my eyes, running through the information in my head one last time. I'm ready for this, I think. I have to be.

The seat next to me shifts as someone settles into it. I open my eyes and there he is.

Ryn.

There are so many empty seats in the classroom. There's no reason for him to sit right next to me. I feel like the butterflies from my father's study have burst from behind the glass and into my chest, their wings flapping.

Begin examination, the hologram flashes.

I lean forward and swipe across the hologram. As I do, Ryn moves toward me. His knee brushes mine. It's nothing more than the slightest whisper, but it sweeps up my spine. The feeling sparkles, spreading under my skin. I turn to look at him. He stares straight ahead, then leans down, swipes the surface of his hologram, and begins moving through each question quickly.

I breathe in and start the test. My hands shake.

The first part is multiple choice. The answers come to me easily, and I barely think as I scan each question.

An hour passes, then one more. I move through math and chemistry, physics and astronomy. Each question is harder than the last. At the end of the astronomy section, I feel myself begin to falter. I read the words in front of me over and over.

List the twenty major characteristics of a pulsar, the last question reads.

I write down ten; then my mind goes blank. There's more, I think. I know there's more. I read through what I have so far, the words repeating in my head.

Small size. High density. Strong magnetic field. Slowing rotation as they age.

My answer is incomplete, but if I don't keep going, I won't finish in time. I move on to the essay, the section of the test with the most impact on the score. I swipe forward and read the question, flinching as I do.

Explain the necessity of Abdolorean intervention on Earth.

My hand hovers over the hologram. We've been taught for all our lives that humans would have destroyed Earth completely if they had been allowed to live, that they hadn't deserved to exist here any longer. My life has been structured around this idea, bent to fit its shape. I know better than to question it, to do anything that could give me away, but my shoulders tense with anger as I write.

Human mistreatment of Earth caused mass environmental devastation, including drastic climate change and the extinction of the majority of the planet's wildlife. With our superior intelligence and advanced technology comes a responsibility to intervene on other planets when necessary. Abdoloreans saved Earth from the destruction caused by a primitive, less evolved species.

I write on and on, scribbling my last sentence just as the holograms fade to black. I lean back in my seat and take a deep breath. They're just words, I tell myself. It's not like writing all that down makes it true.

The hologram lights up, my results flashing across it.

Ninety-five percent.

Relief floods over me; lightness courses through my veins. I did it. I made top five. I stand up and glance at the seat next to me. It's empty. Ryn is already gone.

On the counter in the kitchen is a bowl full of clementines. I take one and peel it, the skin slipping off in one long spiral. I eat one clementine, then another, balancing the rinds on the counter like the rings of a distant planet. I passed the exam. I made top five. If I can keep up during Assessment, I'll have a good chance at making officer. But all I can think about is my jump into the water. All I see is Ryn.

I walk to the window and look out at the water below, replaying yesterday in my head, trying to untangle everything. My memory is hazy, like it all happened to someone else and I was just watching from far away. I see myself making the reckless decision to climb, to jump. I see my breakable human body hitting the water.

Ryn didn't say anything, but that doesn't mean I'm safe. Maybe he realized right away that there was something off about me. Maybe he realized it later that night, thinking about the strange girl whose gills didn't work. Maybe he realized it today, sitting beside me. He could turn me in at any moment. He could be telling the Agency now.

My stomach feels hollow. The quiet of the house unsettles me, my thoughts echoing in the silence. Zo is at school, her classes continuing on their normal schedule. My father is at work. Assessment doesn't start until the end of the week. The day stretches out before me, the hours empty, unbound. I don't know what to do with myself, with the restless energy rushing through me.

I walk through the garden picking mulberries. I lie in the branches of a cherry blossom tree, pressing petals between the palms of my hands. I wander through the house, picking out books from my father's study, reading one after the other lying on the floor of my room. The whole time, a weight presses on my chest, reminding me of the mistake I made.

At one point I look up from my book to see the door holo flashing. My body goes cold. I clench my hands together to stop them from shaking. All I can think is that it's someone from the Agency, coming to take me away. My fear feels entirely rational and irrational all at once.

I stand in the doorway of my room, trying to decide what to do next. The holo flashes again. I walk downstairs, my heart pounding in my chest. I go through the kitchen and stand in front of the door, holding my breath. I press my hand to the glass. The door slides open. I blink in the sunlight.

Ryn stands in front of me, as though I conjured him.

"Ryn," I say, confused. "What are you doing here?"

I look past him to the garden, to the trees surrounding the yard, but there's no one here but him.

"I wanted to see you again," he says, smiling at me. "I waited outside after the exam, but I couldn't find you. I wanted to say hi."

"That's all?" I ask. My pulse flutters. Maybe this happens all the time, boys just showing up at girls' houses for no reason, but it's never happened to me.

"Well, yeah," he says, shrugging. He's wearing a gray shirt, ripped jeans, and black boots.

"Well, hi," I say nervously, wanting to reach up and touch my gills. Instead I cross my arms over my chest.

"Hi." He runs his hands through his silver-blond hair. He looks up to the sun, then back to me, his green eyes clear.

"I'm on my way to the city," he says. "Come with me."

I study his face. I can't read him at all. Maybe he's here for the reasons he said, or maybe he's just as suspicious of me as I am of him.

When I hesitate, he shifts from one foot to the other. "I mean, if you're not interested, or you're with someone—"

I laugh. I can't help it. "It's not that," I promise him.

He smiles, and I can't help smiling back. Before I can overthink anything, I take a deep breath and step through the doorway. There's only one way for me to find out what he knows.

"Okay," I say. "Let's go."

We walk away from the house and into the forest. Sunlight flickers through the branches of the trees, falling across Ryn's face and hands.

"Yesterday was so amazing," he says as we walk. "I haven't been by an ocean in so long."

I glance at him, wondering where he's going with this. If it has anything to do with me.

"My family just moved to Earth," he explains. "I've

been living on Tularu for the past few years. My dad's a commander in the Forces, so I grew up all around the galaxy. We came here so I could get my placement."

A wave of relief floods over me. If Ryn hasn't been on Earth before, he might not know much about humans. He might not know that we can't breathe underwater.

We reach the landing below the station and step up to the chutes rising to the platform. When we get there, Ryn leans against the station wall, looking at the awnings above us.

"What's Tularu like?" I ask, curious. "Aside from not having an ocean."

"The sky is always yellow," he says. "And there are mountains everywhere."

I lean against the wall next to him. "Do you miss it?"

"Not really." He shrugs. "We weren't allowed to go off base much, because of all the civil unrest."

"I didn't know we had a base there at all," I say.

"It's a temporary base, set up as part of the peace-keeping mission," he says. "Well, the Forces call it peacekeeping, but really what they're doing is quelling a revolution."

I blink, not accustomed to hearing anyone talk like this. Abdoloreans don't question their missions.

"What do you mean?" I ask.

"Tularans have had the same leader for almost a

hundred years," he says. "They rose up against her and our government sent in troops, all because we have an alliance with her. It's basically an invasion, just no one's calling it that."

The train rushes into the station and we slide into the seats, facing each other.

"What about you, though?" he asks. "How long have you lived here?"

"My family came right after Repopulation," I say. "We left Abdolora when I was really young. I don't remember anything about it."

I've said this so many times in my life, it almost feels true.

"Do you ever go back?"

I shake my head.

"We go back sometimes," Ryn tells me as the train begins to move. "Whenever my dad needs to report to Mission Control. We never stay very long, though."

I squint into the distance, trying to think of something else to say. The city glitters as it comes into view, its light refracting off the water, splitting into a thousand pieces scattered over the waves.

"What's it like, moving around so much?" I ask him.

"It can be lonely, but I've never known anything else," he says. "I've just learned not to get too used to places."

It strikes me that Ryn and I are alike. He doesn't let

himself get attached to the planets he's lived on, I don't let myself get close to people around me. I've had years of learning how to keep my distance, how to stay apart. Some days it feels like I'm adrift, wandering through the world.

I watch Ryn as he looks down at the water below. I study the way his hands move when he speaks.

"So Conscription isn't such a big deal," I say. "I mean, spending seven years on some random planet isn't so crazy for you."

Ryn shrugs. "That part doesn't bother me," he says.

"There's a part that does?" I ask.

"I'm not so into the idea of being in the Forces at all, really," he says. "I don't believe in a lot of what they do."

I flinch. No one I know has ever said something like this. A lifetime of following the rules, of blending in, of assimilation, wraps around me in cold comfort. No one is near us, but still, the thought that someone could have heard him scares me.

The train pulls into the station and we step off and turn down the street. Ryn moves easily through the crowds, like he barely notices the people around him. He picks two flowers from a honeysuckle vine and hands one to me. I bite into it lightly, the nectar just a drop on my tongue.

"Where are we going?" I ask, suddenly aware that I have no idea where he's taking me.

"You'll see," he says, smiling.

We head to the eastern side of the city, past the shopping center known as the Emporium, farther out to where the buildings edge up against lush open fields. I realize that we're walking to the Biodome, a glass-domed structure that houses the last surviving animals in the Bay. My father used to bring Zo and me here when we were younger. He thought it was important for me to see the way the Earth once was. It always touched me, how he tried to give me glimpses into the past. It was like we were paying our respects to what came before us, to the ways that humans lived.

Ryn and I wander quietly through the exhibits, stopping in front of a field of cows. There are at least a hundred of them scattered across the grass, majestic in their own way. They flick their tails lazily and stomp their hooves in the dirt. I reach up and press my hand against the glass, as though I can touch them, as though I can trace their spots with my fingers.

"I can't believe humans farmed animals the way they did," Ryn says, gazing out at the cows.

I nod, saying nothing, staying neutral. Everyone around us gapes at the cows, murmuring to one another.

"I don't get it at all," he continues. "The essential cruelty of it, the way it completely destroyed the land."

"I don't think they knew any better," I blurt out,

thinking back to the examination. "By the time they figured out how damaged Earth was, they didn't know how to change their ways."

A tall woman standing nearby glares at me. "What are they teaching in school these days?" she mutters under her breath as she wanders off.

Ryn rolls his eyes in solidarity, then tilts his head slightly, and I know he's considering what I've just said. I swallow, hard. It's not like me at all to say how I feel. But something about being with Ryn makes me want to reveal my feelings, to be listened to. Still, maybe I said too much, went too far.

"I mean, I don't think the way they lived was right," I backpedal, my face flushing. "I just think they didn't know how else to exist here, the way we do."

He nods, then touches my arm, the gentle pressure of his fingers lingering on my skin after he takes his hand away.

"Come on," he says. "I want to show you something."

We walk through the entrance of the Ocean Hall, its light blue-tinged and dim. Kelp and starfish line the walls. The room is filled with replicas of animal life, shimmering projections of whales leaping, their songs low and mournful. It feels like we're underwater, back when the ocean was full, before the bomb. Ryn points to a fossil, the imprint of some fish, its skeleton pressed into the slate.

"I wish I knew what it was like to live here before," he says. "It must have been amazing, so many different creatures filling Earth."

I look at the fossil, studying the splay of its fins, the delicate spread of its spine, the empty circle where its eye once was. I know how Ryn feels. I used to dream about living on Earth when there was wildlife, when birds flew through the air and bugs squirmed through the dirt. How magical it must have been, how truly and completely alive.

"They're working on repopulating the ocean," I tell him. "They think in a few years, the radiation will be at low-enough levels that they can reintroduce at least some of the marine life that died out."

Ryn's eyes shine with excitement.

"That's exactly the kind of project I want to be a part of," he says.

"You should do it," I say. "After Conscription, I mean."

His face falls, and he lifts one shoulder in a shrug.

"I don't think so." He sounds defeated.

He's quiet, watching the fossil as if it can move, speak.

"All I've ever wanted is to be a marine biologist," he says finally. "But my dad expects me to do exactly what he's done—become a commander and spend the rest of my life in the Forces. He'd never let me do anything but that."

Ryn's words run through my head. My own life has been so focused on surviving the next seven years that I've barely given any thought to what I'll do after Conscription. Maybe it's because I've never been sure that I'll make it through at all. Don't go there now, I tell myself. Moment by moment. Day after day.

"Have you ever tried to talk to your dad about it?" I ask.

He snorts. "Yeah, but he doesn't care. I don't really have a choice."

"I know how you feel," I sympathize, surprised to find that I actually do. "All my dad cares about is me making officer," I tell him. "I'm not allowed to fail."

The reflection of a school of fish skates across the wall, their fins flickering silver light across Ryn's face. For a moment he looks incandescent, he almost glows. He leans in, closer to me, the space between us disappearing. Our arms touch, and it feels like electricity. It feels like shooting stars.

"I should get back home soon," I say quietly. "My dad will be wondering where I am." I can feel myself on the edge of saying too much. I have to keep my distance, I remind myself. I can't let myself get too close.

Ryn nods, but he doesn't move his arm away.

"Do you want to know what the best part of this place is?" I ask Ryn, not yet willing to leave.

"Um, of course," he says.

I lead him up the winding stairs, all the way to the top floor. The ceiling is rounded, the room one huge, empty circle. This is Zo's favorite place in the Biodome.

"Stand there," I tell him, pointing toward an archway. He leans against the curve of the wall. I walk to the far side of the room, then turn to face him.

"Hello, Ryn," I whisper, and wait.

The words I say reach him a few seconds later. A smile spreads over his face. I close my eyes.

"Hello," his voice whispers a moment later, as though he's standing right next to me. When I open my eyes, he gives me a wave. I raise my hand slowly, waving back.

This boy with silver-blond hair and dark green eyes, who grew up all around the galaxy, is here with me. A girl who, if the truth were known, would be placed in a medical facility and studied by scientists, a living experiment.

He has no idea what I really am, I think, feeling a catch in my throat, wishing at once that the distance between us could be bridged as easily as our voices floating through the air.

six

The next morning I wake before the sun rises. I slip out of bed and walk over to the window. It slides open as I run my hand across the glass. The air feels heavier than usual, or maybe it's just the weight of what today holds, pressing down on me. I walk to my closet and put on the uniform I'll wear for Assessment. It's a silver jumpsuit with the Forces emblem on the chest, a cresting wave made up of stars. I put on my boots and tie the laces tight.

My father is already awake, sitting at the kitchen table. I pour myself a glass of water and sit down across from him, trying to ignore the pressure in my chest.

"Hi, Li," he says. "How are you feeling?"

"Dad," I say, my voice low, "I don't think I can do this."

He reaches out and puts his hands over mine.

"I know you can do this," he says firmly. He sounds so certain. I only wish I felt the same.

"It's just, everything that could happen if I don't make it . . ." My voice wavers. I look down at the floor, the words stuck in my throat.

"You can let fear in," he says softly. "But you can't let it overtake you."

He stands up and walks over to me, pressing a kiss against my forehead.

"You're braver than you think, Li," he says. "You have to trust yourself. Trust that you can do this."

I force myself to smile, like I know he wants me to do, trying to summon the strength he sees in me.

I leave for the train before Zo wakes up, walking alone to the station. The platform is full of other Level Fours, but it's quieter than usual, everyone anticipating the day ahead. None of us knows what to expect. Assessment takes place on a Forces base, along the far edge of the Bay. For the next two months, we'll all go there to perform a series of tests, mental and physical, to establish our ranking and determine our future.

I look out through the waves, all the way to the ocean floor. I can see the ripples of sand that span it, fanning out endlessly. My thoughts float to Ryn. I bite my lip to stop from breaking into a smile.

"How do I look?" Mirabae comes up beside me, her purple hair pulled into a tight topknot. She motions to her uniform, tied at the waist with a belt.

"Amazing," I say, smiling back at her. "Absolutely gorgeous."

The train pulls into the station and an awed silence falls over the platform. The train is just for us. It's silver with circular windows, made up of three different levels. The star-filled wave spans the side of the train. The doors lift and everyone rushes on, sliding into the rows of seats.

Mirabae and I find two seats together. The train pulls away from the platform, picking up speed as we cross the bridge. We move over the ocean, the water churning wildly underneath the tracks. Before long, the base comes into view, unfolding before us. One building looms in the center, surrounded by metallic domes. These are the stations where our testing will take place.

The train pulls up to the platform along the edge of the base and the doors open. In front of each door is a metal archway, scanning us for intake. This is it, I think. No going back now. I step off the train and through the arch. Blue dots of light flash over my body. A line of words appears before me.

I move through the arch and follow Mirabae onto the base. We walk to the auditorium, all of us a sea of silver. Mirabae weaves through the crowd, finding space for us to stand in the middle of the room. I don't see Ryn, but everyone looks so similar in uniform. Magister Sethra stands on a platform before us, her robes a darker silver than our uniforms. She looks at the crowd and we all fall quiet.

"Welcome, Cadets," she says. Her white hair is cut in a sharply angled bob. "Today marks the beginning of your journey as part of the Abdolorean Armed Forces. You are joining an elite group, one that defends freedom and stability across the galaxy."

A cheer breaks out across the room. I force myself to join in, smiling and clapping along with everyone else.

"For the next eight weeks, you'll learn about the planets you might visit as members of the Forces. You'll learn about the tactics the Forces deploy, and you will go through rigorous physical training to prepare you for service."

Mirabae looks at me, her eyes shining with excitement. I know she's thinking of all the places she wants to go, the way the galaxy will open up around her. She doesn't know what it feels like to be scared of her future.

I glance around the room, looking for Ryn again. This time I find him, looking straight at me. He smiles and my stomach swoops to the ground.

"A major part of your training includes practice simulations. During each simulation, you will be placed in situations you might encounter during service, each one harder than the last. These practice simulations are meant to prepare you for your final simulation examination, upon which your placement is decided."

This much we already know, but each year, the sims change, making it impossible to anticipate what we'll be tested on. We won't learn anything about them until the moment before each one begins.

Sethra's voice softens. "As you all know, Assessment ends not only with your placements, but with the farewell gala, to commemorate your accomplishments and celebrate all your hard work before Conscription begins."

The gala is legendary, a night when everyone dresses up and dances, a night when everyone goes wild. I should be excited about it, like everyone else, but all it does is fill me with anxiety. After the gala, there's only a week before we leave the Bay, before our lives change completely.

"Your official training will begin tomorrow. In accordance with the Forces mandate, you will be placed in a seven-person unit, which you will work with for the duration of Assessment," Sethra says. "During your simulations, one cadet from each unit will act as leader. In a moment, you will receive your unit numbers. These numbers also correspond to the simulation station to which you are assigned."

She clasps her hands in front of her, the rings she wears catching the light.

Our assignments appear in the air before us, the words flashing blue, sparkling.

Cadet Li: Unit Fifteen.

I'm with Braxon, Nava, Ranthu, Akia, Mirabae . . . and Ryn. Involuntarily, my eyes flicker to Ryn across the room. He offers a broad smile and my skin tingles.

"You will meet up with your unit tomorrow. For now, you're all dismissed to tour the facility and get your bearings."

Everyone streams out of the auditorium, a murmur of anticipation in the air. So much is unknown. I feel like I have to do something to help my chances.

"I'll see you later," I say to Mirabae, and walk toward Magister Sethra with an air of confidence I don't really feel.

"Magister Sethra," I call. "Do you have a moment to talk?"

She turns to me. "Of course," she says. "Let's go to my office."

We walk through the hall behind the auditorium,

down to the lowest level of the building. She stops in front of a door, pressing her hand against it. The door opens, revealing a room with a desk, two chairs, and maps of the galaxies covering the walls. Sethra swipes her hand across the maps and they all fade to black. A pitcher of rose water sits on her desk, two glasses beside it. She pours the rose water into the glasses and hands one to me.

"Now," she says. "What's on your mind?"

"I hope you know that I've always worked my hardest," I say, clasping my hands tightly around the glass.

Sethra smiles and sits back in her chair, crossing her legs, her robes flowing around her. "I do know this, Cadet Li." She narrows her eyes at me, as if she can read my thoughts.

"I'm wondering . . ." I swallow. "Is there anything else I can do to secure a place as officer?"

"Your chances of ranking in an officer position are very good so far," she tells me. I feel a rush of relief. "You should know, though, that the competition will not be easy. Your score on the final was tied with another student, placing the two of you in direct competition for the position."

"Who?" I ask, before I can stop myself.

"Cadet Braxon," she says, and my heart sinks. Of course it's him. "Now, he hasn't spoken with me, so he doesn't know you're his main competition." She smiles.

"Coming to meet with me has given you some extra insight that you can use to your advantage, Cadet Li."

I force myself to smile. "I'll try, Magister Sethra."

"My advice is to avoid all distractions. I believe you have what it takes to make officer," she says, standing to open the door. She puts her hand on my shoulder. "Prove me right."

I take the train home with Mirabae and Akia. I look out the window, smiling and nodding as they talk about the day. I can't stop thinking about what Magister Sethra said . . . or who I'm up against. I walk into the house and collapse onto the couch, waiting for the stress of the day to fade away.

"Li!" Zo calls from the doorway of her room. "I've been waiting for you!"

She runs down the stairs. Her cheeks are flushed and her eyes shine.

"You're never going to guess what happened," she says breathlessly. "I saw Braxon on my way home. He's getting some people together to celebrate Assessment and he invited me. You have to come."

"He's throwing a party tonight?" I ask incredulously, though I shouldn't be surprised. "On the first night of Assessment?"

"It's not a *party*," she corrects me, looking apprehensive. "It's just a few people hanging out."

I hear Sethra's words in my head, telling me to concentrate.

"I don't think it's a good idea," I say uneasily. "Training starts tomorrow, and it's going to be intense."

Zo puts her hands on her hips, her eyes pleading. "I'd do it for you. Come with me, please."

"I don't know, Zo," I say slowly.

She flops down on the couch next to me, giving me the look she always gives me when she wants me to do something for her, arching her eyebrows and smiling.

"You don't know, as in, yes, you'll definitely come?"

I sigh. Zo has had to give up so much for me, it's hard not to feel guilty. If it weren't for me, she'd have a normal Abdolorean life, with a father who wasn't consumed with worry, always thinking up new physical challenges and trials to test me. Before I can say anything, she throws her arms around me.

"You're the best," she says into my neck, her breath warm on my useless gills. "This is going to be awesome, you'll see. I promise you won't regret it."

We wait until midnight, then slip downstairs and out the back door. We cut across the forest, slinking through the trees to the far end of the Bay. Our feet press against the mossy earth, and our clothes catch the light of the moon. The trees part to reveal a small stretch of beach. Braxon's house sits at the edge of the shore, raised high above the water. I look through the windows, my heart sinking. There are at least a hundred kids here, laughing and shouting, dancing around the house.

I follow Zo inside. Glowing orbs are strung along the ceiling, playing music, their light flashing with the beat. The floors are made of glass, like we're standing on top of the ocean itself. Almost at once, Zo disappears into the crowd. I stand along the edge of the room, searching for someone I know. From a distance, I see the flash of Mirabae's hair. I'm about to walk over to her when Braxon comes up beside me.

"Li," he says. "I didn't think you'd make it."

"I made it," I say, watching as Mirabae slips out the door, following Cailei onto the beach.

"I'm glad you did," he says. "I like seeing you around."

He takes a step closer and slips his arm around my waist, his fingers brushing my hip.

"I wouldn't mind seeing more of you," he says, running his hand down my body. I step away from him, untangling myself from his grasp.

"Zo's here somewhere," I say, my voice pointed.

Braxon's eyes flicker, a shadow passing over them. He smiles at me, but something about it is sharp and insincere. He reaches into his pocket and holds his hand out, a translucent tab of Kala in his palm.

"You want some?" he asks.

Kala enhances Abdolorean senses, making them even more intense. Colors grow brighter, shapes change form, every sound grows louder, deeper. At least, that's what I've heard. I've never taken it. I don't know what it could do to me.

"No, I'm good," I say.

Braxon shrugs. "Your loss, Cadet."

He pops the tab into his mouth. Almost at once, his eyes start to glow. I look across the room. All around me, people dance wildly, their eyes closed, their arms up, their bodies pressed together. Outside, people swim in the water, splashing through the waves. Everyone here is on Kala, I realize. Everyone except me.

"I'll see you later," I tell him, and walk away. I have to find Zo. We need to go.

I move through the crush of bodies, searching for Zo, finding her nowhere. I'm about to go look for her outside when I hear someone call my name.

I turn around and see Ryn leaning against the wall. I peer into his eyes to see if he's on Kala, but they're the same green as always.

"Hey, you," he says.

"Oh. Hey," I say, a smile escaping my lips.

Ryn looks around the room, disbelief on his face. "This is pretty crazy."

The music swells. Everyone is shouting, throwing their hands up in the air.

"Yeah," I say over the music. "It's not really my thing."

Ryn nods, taking in the chaos around us. "Do you want to get out of here?"

"Yes," I say. How simple that word is, I think. How good it feels to say.

We walk down the beach until we reach an old train bridge. We climb up the beams and sit on the tracks, letting our feet dangle over the edge. Ryn looks up at the sky, tapping his knee against mine.

"If you could be anywhere right now, where would you be?" he asks. I think about the places this galaxy holds, all the planets, all their moons, and find that there's only one place I really want to be.

"With Zo in our garden." We would lie by the hydrangea bushes like we used to when we were younger, shaking off their petals and pretending it was snow. "How about you?"

"Karabdis," he says. "We lived there for a few years when I was younger. Its ocean has these bioluminescent starfish that light up when you touch them. It's how they scare off predators. It's one of the most amazing things I've ever seen."

I look at the dark, empty water before us and wonder what it was like to swim surrounded by those starfish, their neon glow pulsing, alive.

"You'll miss her a lot when we leave for placement," Ryn says. "Your sister, I mean."

"I really will," I say, more to myself than to him. "I won't see her for seven years. Eight years, really, after her Conscription. We'll be entirely different people by the time we come back."

Ryn swings his legs slowly and looks down at his hands.

"I was happy when my brother left," he admits, lifting his shoulders in the slightest shrug. "We aren't close. We can barely even be in the same room."

He stares at the stars like he's waiting to see something, but all they do is glow.

"He was never nice, even when we were kids. I mean, he was nice enough to me, he just ignored me most of the time. But I would see the way he treated other people, like he was so much better than them."

I study his profile, the focused look in his eyes. "How so?"

"It's not that he's cruel or mean. It's more that he's

distant. Cold. He holds himself apart from everyone else, including me. By the time he left, I didn't even miss him. It was like he was already gone." Ryn takes a breath and lets it out slowly. He shakes his head. "I used to feel bad about it, not liking my own brother."

"What changed?" I ask. I can't imagine my world without Zo. I know how lonely that world would be. Maybe she and I are closer than other siblings are. Maybe our secrets have bound us in different, unbreakable ways.

"I did, I guess," Ryn says. "We grew even further apart when he was gone. He was placed on Utula and never left. He's working his way from officer to commander, just like my dad wants." The tiny muscle under Ryn's eye twitches.

"You don't have to be like your brother," I say softly, remembering what we talked about yesterday. "Or your dad."

"I'm not sure it's that easy." He looks into the distance; then his gaze flits back to me. "Let's swim," he says suddenly. "Let's go, right now."

He jumps down from the bridge, then smiles up at me, his face full of light.

"You coming?" he asks, and I can't help but smile back.

"Are you trying to distract me from this intense and

depressing conversation about our families?" I laugh, then jump, stumbling slightly as I land. Ryn reaches out to steady me, his hands on my hips. His fingers press against my skin, just under the hem of my shirt.

"Sorry," he apologizes. He drops his hands, but still I feel their warmth on my skin.

"That's okay."

We stare at each other until I break eye contact. He pulls off his shirt, dropping it onto the shore. Moonlight falls onto the hollows of his collarbones, spreading across his chest. He dives below the surface of the waves. I strip down to my underwear and run into the water, swimming out to meet him. We float on our backs, staring up at the sky.

"I thought about staying on Tularu," Ryn says, breaking the silence between us. "Just skipping Assessment altogether."

He moves his arms and the water ripples around us.

"Defecting, you mean?"

Ryn smiles. "Not defecting, really. More like disappearing into the mountains and never coming back."

"So why didn't you?" I ask, turning to look at him.

"I didn't want to have to hide for the rest of my life."

I know how you feel, I think, but say nothing at all. He closes his eyes, and I wonder if he's imagining a life in the mountains. I wonder if he's thinking of me.

"I'm happy I'm here, though," he says. "I'm happy I came."

He opens his eyes, looking up at the sky again.

"I thought you hated this," I say.

He grins.

"Not all of it," he says.

seven

For the rest of the week, there are no more parties. I throw myself into training, leaving early each morning to go to base, staying late each night. I see Ryn at training and tactics class, but I try to stay focused. I feel myself grow stronger with each passing day, my muscles tight, my body powerful.

The walls of the compound are lined with targets shaped like bodies. A gun rests by each one. Conditioning stations fill the room, stacks of free weights and circuit machines. This late in the afternoon, the compound is mostly empty. Only a few other cadets move through the stations.

Along the ceiling is a series of metal bars hanging at

different heights. I climb up to the platform beneath them and walk to the edge. I reach up and grab the first bar. I breathe in and push my feet off the platform, taking flight. I swing in the air, finding an easy rhythm; then I let go, stretching my arms out in front of me. I catch hold of the next bar. My palms sting, but I tighten my grip. I don't let go. I fly from one bar to the next, spinning in the air until everything blurs away.

I reach the last bar and pull myself up, curl my legs around it, and flip my body over. I hang there, swaying, the world upside down and strange, then straighten my legs and fall. I land in a crouch, my heart pounding, my feet firmly on the ground.

I look across the room. Ryn and Mirabae stand together at one of the conditioning stations, lifting weights high above their heads. I walk over to meet them.

"Hey," Mirabae says, working to catch her breath. She drops her weights to the floor. "I asked Ryn to help me train."

"Is there anything in particular you want to work on?" Ryn asks her. I've noticed that Mirabae hasn't been as confident as she usually is. The week has been harder than she expected. All the years of training with my father have prepared me completely. I'm used to intense physical activity; I'm mentally prepared for the challenges we'll face.

"Combat tactics," she says. "I need to be able to protect myself better."

Ryn lifts the weights from the ground and puts them back in their place. He's stronger than he seems, I realize, watching the easy way his body moves.

"Let's start with some target practice," he says. "Get you used to handling a gun. Li, you in?"

"Sure," I say, and together we walk over to the targets. Ryn picks up a gun and shoots a line of bullets straight down the target, from head to neck to chest. I shoot just once. The bullet hits right where the heart would be. Mirabae aims her gun at the target, but it's unsteady in her hands. The bullets hit the body in the shoulder, the neck.

"Not bad," Ryn says. "Try again. Aim for the chest."

He stands beside her, showing her exactly how to point the gun. The next shot she takes hits the body right in the middle of the chest.

"Nice," he says, clapping. "See how much better you are already?"

Mirabae flushes happily, bringing her gun up to shoot again.

"Do you want to know the secret to making all your shots?" Ryn asks. "Deep breaths and mindfulness, but mostly deep breaths. Always make sure you're calm before you shoot."

Mirabae laughs. "Seems a little contradictory."

"Let's not worry about semantics," he says. "We'll just work on making you a better shot for now."

She keeps shooting, each shot a little better than the last.

Next we follow him to the mats. He rolls up the sleeves of his uniform and puts his fists in front of his face, bouncing lightly on his toes. He shows Mirabae the right way to hold her fists, how to get her weight behind her while throwing a punch.

"Always go forward, never retreat," Ryn tells us. "That's the most important defense tactic there is. Moving backward gives your opponent a chance to get into your space, to really get at you."

They circle each other, Mirabae stepping close enough to land a punch on his shoulder. He steps back and drops his arms, surprised, and she swipes at him again. She hits him across the other shoulder, then again in the chest, and Ryn throws his hands up in the air.

"That was good," he says. "I surrender."

Mirabae drops her fists, her arms loose at her sides.

"You," he says, pointing to me. "Get over here."

I stand in front of him, my fists up. I throw out a light punch, catching him against the side of his arm. He reaches out and grabs my wrist. He steps back, and I stick my foot behind his. He falls backward, pulling me down with him. I lie on top of him, our faces nearly touching.

"Never retreat, remember?" I say breathlessly. "I took you down."

"Yeah," he says. "But I took you with me."

He puts his hands over my hips, shifting my body off his. He sits up and rests his arms across his knees.

"You realize I'm still here, right?" Mirabae says, laughing.

My face flushes. I stand up and reach my hand out to Ryn. He grabs hold of it and pulls himself up. Mirabae catches my eye and smiles.

Ryn stretches his arms above his head. "I think that's enough for today."

"Thanks, both of you, for real," Mirabae says. "I feel so much better than I did before."

"Anytime, Mir." Ryn smiles.

She swings her pack onto her shoulders. "I'm heading home," she says. "See you two tomorrow."

Ryn looks at me. "Do you have anywhere you need to be?" he asks, and I shake my head.

"Good," he says. "Because there's somewhere I want to take you."

He takes my hand, and I feel the subtle beat of his pulse, the heat of his skin against mine.

We walk across the base until we reach a slice of beach surrounded by trees. Their branches stretch out over the ocean, bursting with flowers. Petals cover the sand and float across the surface of the water. We could be on some undiscovered planet, someplace far from here. Ryn walks to the edge of the water and gathers a handful of petals, pale pink, holding them out to me.

"We lived on Vesunia for a few years when I was a kid," he says. "The whole planet is covered in these trees."

"They're magnolias," I say, taking the petals from his hands.

Ryn smiles. "Vesunians call these trees Hinthia," he says. "It means 'soul of the dead.' Everyone there is born with white hair, and when they turn seventeen they go off alone for a month. When they come back, they dye their hair pink with these flowers, marking the end of their youth."

"What happens if they don't survive the month?" I ask.

"Their body is burned to ash and buried at the base of a tree," he says.

We walk barefoot along the edge of the shore. The petals part as we move slowly through them.

"So it's a life-or-death ritual," I say. "That's intense."

"It's not that different from what we do, really," Ryn says. "We get sent away from our homes, out to some other planet. We have no guarantee that we'll survive, either."

He leads me away from the water, over to one of the trees. We sit in the curve of its branches, our bodies close together.

"You're a good fighter," I say. "You know what you're doing. You'll be able to survive."

"You too," he says.

I can't tell him that I've worked every day of my life just to stay alive. "Where did you learn to fight like that?" I ask instead.

"My father taught me combat skills when I was pretty young," he says. "He wanted me to be prepared, I guess."

"Mine too, actually," I say. "Sometimes I feel like it's the only thing I know."

This is the closest thing to the truth about myself that I'll ever be able to share with Ryn. A certain kind of sadness fills me. I think about the things I want, the things that I can't have. Ryn's leg brushes against mine, and I wonder, just for a moment, how it would feel to tell him everything.

"Do you ever think about dying?" I ask, my voice quiet.

"Of course," he says. "Especially now. Don't you?"

I nod, feeling the beat of my heart through my bones.

"I worry more about being captured by the enemy," I say. "Living the rest of my life being tortured, or something like that."

My mind flashes to Ava, bound to her bed, her body used and discarded, death the only thing that freed her.

"That would be terrifying," he says. "But you're strong enough to survive that."

"I hope I would be," I say, and I can't meet his eyes.

He lifts his hand to my chin, tilting my face toward his. "I bet you could survive anything." He leans forward, his lips parted.

I close my eyes, resting my hand on his chest, breathing in.

I pull back.

I know what comes next.

"I have to go," I say, my voice barely above a whisper.

Ryn drops his hand from my cheek, his fingers trailing slowly over my skin. Together, we climb down from the tree. He reaches up and pulls a blossom from a branch. We walk back across base and board the train, the air around us electric, alive. Just after we leave the station, before we head home, Ryn takes my hand and presses the flower into it.

"How did training go today?" Zo asks that night as we walk through the garden, gathering food for dinner. Every house in the Bay has a garden, a small plot of land given to each family by the government. The gardens are part of the Cultivation Enrichment Program. Each household is responsible for its own food source, just one more step forward in Abdolorean innovation.

Our father taught us how to plant seeds in long lines, leaving space for them to grow. The seeds are all genetically enhanced, and they bloom within a week of planting. I wander through the twisted vines, picking peaches, my bare feet buried in the dirt. Zo trails behind me, eating tomatoes like apples.

"It was fine," I tell her. "We worked on some strength exercises."

Zo bends down and picks a bunch of carrots. I walk through the rows of snow peas, snapping them from their vines. My muscles are sore, but in a good way, like I'm working hard at something and succeeding, as if Ryn were still nearby. It's a feeling I could get used to.

We go through the entire garden, then head back into the house, pulling plates from the shelves, setting our food down on the table.

"Do you want these?" Zo asks, pushing a plate of grapes toward me. "They're too sweet for me."

"You're the only person I know who likes their grapes sour," I say, picking one off the stem and popping it into my mouth.

"So," she says, tilting her head to one side. "How are things with Ryn?"

"What do you mean?" I ask, my breath hitching in my chest.

She smiles and raises her eyebrows. "Are you guys chatting? Do you want him to *call* you?" she teases, using the word humans once used. Abdoloreans don't use the same technology my ancestors did. To reach someone now, you beam them—your silhouette appears in the air in front of them, and they can choose to engage with you or not.

My cheeks flush. I run my finger along the edge of the table.

"Do you like him?" she asks. I feel her watching me, and I keep my face blank. I want to tell her everything. But I know I shouldn't feel anything for him. Just being near him is dangerous.

"No," I lie. "He's in my Assessment group, that's all."

"That's too bad," she says. "It's pretty nice, liking someone and having them like you back."

I know she's waiting for me to ask her what she means. When I don't, she leans over and stares at me until I look up at her.

"Braxon kissed me," she says, pulling off a grape and tossing it at me. I've never seen her look so happy. "The night of the party. He said he's never met anyone like me before. He said I'm amazing."

I nod slowly, remembering the way he touched me that night, holding on to me just because he could.

"Be careful, Zo," I say.

"What's that supposed to mean?" she asks, a shadow passing over her face.

"Exactly what it sounds like." I shrug. "Braxon isn't a good guy, that's all."

She leans back in her chair, her eyes flashing.

"What's your problem?" she asks. "Why can't you be happy for me?" She pushes her chair back from the table.

"Zo," I say, my voice calm. "I'm just saying I'd be careful if I were you. He barely knows you; how can he say he's never met anyone like you?"

"It's like all you want is for us both to be miserable," Zo scoffs, her chin quivering. A wave of guilt washes over me.

Before I can apologize, she goes on. "Unlike you, I don't have to be alone for the rest of my life."

I flinch as though she's reached out and slapped me.

The color leaves her face as she realizes what she's said. She opens her mouth, as though to say something more, then changes her mind, turning and leaving me by myself.

eight

For days after our fight, Zo and I are still circling each other, moving from room to room without speaking, looking away when we pass each other in the hall. I'm distracted at training later that week when a man I don't recognize stands beside Magister Sethra, his uniform a darker version of the ones we have on, signifying his rank as officer.

"Attention, Cadets," Sethra says. Everyone stops talking and turns to her. "Special Forces Officer Veku will be leading you in a tactical training workshop today," she tells us. "You are to give him your full attention."

She turns and moves to the edge of the room. Officer

Veku steps forward and clears his throat. Ryn looks down the line, catching my eye.

Hi, he mouths.

Hi, I mouth back.

We've spent the whole week together. Each day, I tell my father a new lie about where I am after Assessment. I feel distance growing between us, a distance he doesn't even know exists. I come home after Zo is in bed, her lights out. Some nights I stand at her doorway, listening for the sound of her inside, but it's always quiet. I wonder if she misses me the way I miss her.

"Today we'll be going over camouflage and tracking techniques," Officer Veku says. "We'll start with aquatic methods for achieving crypsis."

The lights dim and a projection of an ocean appears around us, full of coral, schools of fish, and sea anemones. Our uniforms shift from silver to blue, matching the color of the water. We walk around the room, exploring the teeming life before us. It feels almost real, like we're actually seeing these creatures, like they're here with us.

"Your uniforms utilize active camouflage technology," Veku explains. "In this way, you already have an advantage over whomever you're trying to hide from."

Ryn comes up next to me, his uniform shimmering as it blends into the water projection. He brushes his hand against mine, and heat races through me, filling me up.

"There are three main camouflage techniques in water," Veku goes on. "Reflection, counterillumination, and transparency."

A school of fish swims past us, scales glittering, and our uniforms shift again to match them, as though our bodies are mirrored, reflecting the light of the sun.

"Fish do this in shallow water," Ryn whispers, looking down at his arms in amazement. "Their scales catch the light and beam it back up to the surface so they blend in with the water. It's called silvering."

The room darkens as though night has fallen. Moonlight shines across the water. The color on our uniforms deepens, giving off a slight glow. I look across the room at Nava and Ranthu, their bodies barely visible in the projection of the water.

"Counterillumination is a method of camouflage in which light is produced to match the illumination of the ocean's surface," Veku says. "Imagine you're stranded at sea and enemy airships are searching for you. If you're being pursued while counterilluminating, you'll blend into the surface of the water, reaching the height of crypsis."

The hologram shifts from night back to day, from ocean to forest. Sunlight filters through the trees. A small stream runs down the middle of the room.

"We'll now go over tracking skills," Veku says. He takes us through the trees, pointing out footsteps in the dirt, broken sticks, and overturned rocks. He shows us subtle marks in the moss, indentations in the vines wrapped around the trees.

"These are all markers of displacement," he says. "Proof that someone walked through here before us."

He shows us how to look for where someone might be hiding, how to move in ever-widening circles if we lose our trail, how to walk through water so our presence can't be traced. He teaches us to use the forest to shield ourselves, how to hide in the underbrush to evade capture, our bodies blending in with the ground.

There are so many ways that this earth can hide us, I think.

There are so many ways to disappear.

The trees around us fade. The lights in the auditorium come up and we're back standing in the middle of an empty room. Magister Sethra waits by the door. She motions for us to follow her outside. The sky is expansive, full of light. After what we just did, the world we're in almost doesn't feel real.

"You're dismissed for the day," Sethra tells us.

Ryn looks over at me hopefully, but today, I shake my head. I promised my father we would train tonight. I know he's worried, and I can't help but think of how much more worried he'd be if he saw the way Ryn and I are smiling at each other now.

*　*　*

"Close your eyes," my father says later that night. "Follow the sound of my voice."

I'm standing on a branch on one of the tallest trees in the forest. The sky is dark, the wind still, the stars just beginning to emerge.

We've been coming to the forest for as long as I remember, training in secret. It's exhausting for me, but I know it's exhausting for my father, too—every hour of sleep I miss to train, he misses as well. Every time I can't get to the place he wants me to reach, he worries as much as I do.

"Are you ready?" His voice floats past.

I inhale deeply and exhale slowly. My lungs press against my ribs. I see Ryn before me, then Zo looking at me with anger in her eyes. But I clear my mind, until I feel like I don't exist. When I was younger, it took me entire days to get to this place, to think of nothing at all. *First breath, then body,* my father would say. *Let the world in and listen to what it's telling you. Listen, then let it go.*

The branch sways with the weight of my body. I'm high above the earth, but I keep my eyes closed, feeling the pulse of the darkness around me.

"I'm ready," I say.

I trace in my mind the space I'm in, the outline of my

body against the sky. I take a step forward. The branch shakes beneath me. I spread my arms out for balance, but it's not enough. My feet slip. I fall through the air and land hard on my back.

My father stands above me, staring down. "You're not focused," he says sharply.

"Yes I am," I say, my jaw clenched.

"Not enough," he says. "Get up. Do it again."

I push myself off the ground, brushing the dirt from my legs. I climb the tree once again, going back to where I started. I close my eyes, determined. The bark cuts into the soles of my feet, but I barely feel it. I imagine spinning from branch to branch, picture myself flying. I will my body to move forward, but it stays frozen in place.

"What's wrong?" My father sounds far away.

"Nothing's wrong," I say, but I can't slow the beat of my heart. I focus my gaze on the air in front of me. The wind rushes past, threatening to push me over. I drop to the ground, standing in front of my father, unable to meet his eyes.

"I've been thinking about what it would be like if things were easier," I say slowly. "What everything would be like if I weren't human."

I've never said this to him before. I've barely let myself think it.

"But you *are* human, Li," he says.

"What if I don't make officer?" I ask quietly. "What happens then?"

It's a subject we've avoided, even though it's all I think about.

"You can't think like that, Li," he says.

I close my eyes. "How can I not?"

"Because you have no choice."

I take a breath, holding it deep in my lungs.

"Li," he says, and I look up. He puts his hand over his heart. "You have to push through whatever it is that's holding you back. I know this is difficult, but you can't give up now."

I look up to the sky through the leaves of the trees. It was all so much easier before, back when there was nothing to distract me, when I didn't know Ryn existed.

"I do want to make it," I say. "It's all I want." I close my eyes as I say this, hoping it sounds true.

"Then do the work," my father bids, motioning to the forest around me.

I wish I could tell him about the other things I want, things from the world that have nothing to do with making officer. We've always worked together as a team; we've never had secrets between us before. But I can't tell my father how I'm feeling. He'd say there was too much on the line, that the risks are too high. And maybe he'd be right.

I climb the tree, my muscles tense with concentration. Sweat beads on the back of my neck. My human mother carried me like a seed inside her, but it is my father, here, who taught me to survive.

I take another breath; I let everything go.

"Li," my father calls up to me. "Jump."

I do as he says. I jump.

My hands reach for the branch above me. My body is a thousand moving parts working together to carry me through the air. The world is a blur around me. I spin through the sky, faster and faster, until my mind is clear.

I land on the ground, triumphant.

nine

On the morning of our first practice sim, our unit meets in front of our simulation station. Some unknown adventure exists beyond those doors, and even though I know it's only a simulation—it's not *real*—my heart beats faster in anticipation. By the time I arrive, the rest of my unit is already here. Braxon leans against the side of the station, its chrome surface gleaming. Nava pulls her hair into a ponytail. Ranthu shifts from one foot to the other, his body tall, lanky. Akia crouches on her heels, tightening the laces on her boots. Ryn and Mirabae stand together. Ryn stretches his arms above his head. A smile crosses his lips as he sees me walk up. I'm too nervous to smile back.

Mirabae flashes me a look, biting her lip, and I can tell how anxious she is. Before I can say anything to her, Magister Sethra walks up to the station and we shift into line before her.

"Attention, Unit Fifteen," she says. She pauses, looking us over, her gaze falling on me. "As commendation for her high score on the academic exam, Cadet Li will be leading you through your mission today."

Everyone turns to look at me. It takes a moment for Sethra's words to sink in. I feel a rush of pride, until I glance over at Braxon, who's looking me up and down, his mouth set in a thin line. I can tell he expected to be leader, and he's used to getting what he wants. My fight with Zo flashes through my mind and I shake it away.

"Cadet Li, Magister's favorite," Braxon says quietly. He smiles like he's joking, but there's a clear edge to his voice. I decide to ignore him, turning to the rest of the unit instead.

"When we get in there," I say, "communication will be our most important tactic."

"How do you know what's most important if we don't even know what the sim is yet?" Braxon asks coolly.

"No matter what the sim is, we have to talk to one another," I say, meeting his gaze. "We have to be in this together, or we all fail."

Braxon rolls his eyes, but he doesn't say anything

more. He's jealous, I tell myself, but he'll listen to me once we get in there. He has to follow my lead, or he'll risk failing the sim.

Magister Sethra turns and presses her hand against the door. We stand behind her in an uneasy silence, none of us knowing what to expect.

The door to the station lifts up. Bright light surrounds us as we move forward. The room is empty, the ceiling and walls an incandescent white.

"It's like we're on the moon," Nava murmurs.

Magister Sethra leads us into the center of the room.

"In this sim, you will be placed on a hostile planet where a rebellion has formed against our presence," she says. "Your orders are to capture the rebel leader, thereby defusing the rebellion itself."

I listen to her carefully, searching her words for clues, realizing quickly that my biggest challenge as leader is that I won't know what to do until we're in the sim.

"You are to avoid casualties at all cost, but remember— sometimes a few must be sacrificed for the greater good. You will be graded not only on the tactics you employ, but also on the speed with which you complete this mission."

Anxious energy fills me, rushing through my veins.

Without another word, Magister Sethra moves to the edge of the room. The lights go down. The walls turn black. When the lights come back up, we're standing in the desert, red sand swirling harshly around us. Our uniforms shift from silver to red, a kind of built-in camouflage.

"This is so cool," Akia says, holding her arms out in front of her.

I look out across the desert, trying to get a sense of where we are. The sun beats mercilessly down on us. There are no caves, no trees; there's nowhere for us to take cover. A settlement of tents sits in the distance, scattered across the sand. This is the rebel encampment. This is our target.

At my feet are our supplies. I sort through them quickly. There are flares, canisters of gas, protective masks, weapons I've never seen before, let alone handled. Buried underneath everything is a small pile of guns. My stomach twists, but there's no time for me to stop and think. I toss a gun, a mask, and a canister out to everyone, keeping a set for myself. I sling my gun across my shoulder and pull the mask down so it hangs around my neck. Everyone looks at me expectantly. I take a deep breath.

"We're going to split into groups," I say, hoping I sound authoritative. "The first group is going to scout the encampment. The second will hang back as reserves. I'll head up the first group. I need two of you to come with me. Any volunteers?"

"I will," Ryn says, his voice calm.

"I'm in, too," Braxon seconds. I hold back a sigh of frustration. I shouldn't be surprised.

"Come in only if you see you the signal," I tell the others.

They all nod. I turn to Ryn and Braxon.

"Let's go."

We race down the dunes, fanning out around the first tent we see. Ryn presses his body to the side of the tent, pushing the flap open with the tip of his gun. He looks at me and shakes his head. We move to the next tent. Braxon peers inside.

"Empty," he says.

We go from tent to tent, each one empty. The camp is eerily quiet. The rebels are nowhere to be found.

"What is this, some kind of trick exam?" Braxon scoffs.

Panic rises in my chest. We've been on our mission for only a few minutes. We can't fail this quickly.

"Let's retrace our steps," I say. I start walking toward the front of the encampment, but Braxon and Ryn stay where they are.

"No one's here," Braxon says. "Retracing our steps isn't going to help us at all."

I look over at Ryn for support, but he's staring out into the distance.

"Li . . . ," he says, pointing past the tents.

A cloud of sand rises up in the air, billowing out, rushing toward us. The wind picks up. The sandstorm races forward at a terrifying speed. It will be on us in seconds and there's nowhere for us to go, no place to hide.

"Masks up!" I shout, my heart pounding. "Get down now."

We drop to the ground. The storm swells, surging over us, blocking out the sun. Sand hits my skin, searing pinpricks across my body. I clench my eyes shut, praying that the storm will pass quickly, that the rest of the unit is okay.

The dust clears. I stagger to my feet and look toward the dunes. I can't see Nava, Akia, Ranthu, or Mirabae, but going back to find them could compromise the mission. My eyes sweep across the perimeter of the camp. At the edge is a tent set back from the rest, one I couldn't see before.

I motion to Ryn and Braxon to follow me, hoping that Braxon won't argue. We creep toward it, keeping low to the ground. I move around to the side of the tent, peeking through an open fold. The rebels are here, all together. They stand around a long table, maps laid out in front of them. Their pale skin is stretched over the sharp bones of their faces. They don't speak. Their hands flutter, moving rapidly, forming signals I don't understand. I don't know what they're saying to one another, if they're planning some kind of attack. We can wipe them out all at once, but our only choice is to storm the tent.

I signal for Ryn and Braxon to pull back. I raise my arm above my head, then let it drop. Ryn sets off the flare. It shoots silently into the air, bursting into a quick flash of light. Nava, Akia, Ranthu, and Mirabae run down the dunes, their faces stained red with sand. Mirabae struggles to breathe, her gills flickering rapidly, her chest heaving with the sheer effort of pulling in air.

"We got caught in the sandstorm," Akia whispers. "She couldn't get her mask down in time."

There's fear in Mirabae's eyes, but we don't have time to be afraid. I point her, Nava, and Akia to one side of the tent; I point Ryn and Ranthu to the other. I point to Braxon, then to the tent's entrance, where there will surely be guards waiting, hoping he'll back off me as long as he gets the chance to show his strength. I walk around to the back of the tent, pressing my body against it, looking at the other cadets, and nodding, once, for everyone to move.

We rush the tent. The rebels scatter away from the table. We pull down our masks and open the canisters of gas, throwing them through the air. The gas hisses, a thick green haze settling around us, making it impossible to see. I hear the dull sound of the rebels' bodies hitting the ground, their ragged breath. Their bodies seize and shudder until finally they're still.

The air clears, revealing a smaller group of rebels with masks of their own. They surround their leader in a tight circle. We have no chance of capturing him without combat.

"Move, now!" I shout, and we descend upon them. We're outnumbered, but we're better fighters than the rebels. I wrestle one to the ground, shoving my gun against her chest, pinning her down. I pull off her mask. She opens her mouth, shrieking, her teeth black. She twitches beneath me. Her eyes roll back into her head; then her body goes limp.

Guilt surges through me, but before I can think about it, I see Ranthu retreating to the edge of the tent, cradling his arm against his chest, his face twisted with pain. I've never seen an Abdolorean injured before. It almost never happens; their bodies are stronger than mine, more resistant to attack.

I move toward him to see if he's okay, when screams split the air. Akia stands in the center of the tent, frozen in place. A rebel races toward her, teeth bared. Braxon leaps out in front of her, smashing his gun across the rebel's forehead, knocking him out. The rebel crumples to the ground, his blood seeping into the sand.

Ryn and Nava sneak around the edge of the tent,

running up behind the last standing rebels. Together, they take them all down, until only their leader is standing. Ryn kicks the leader's legs out from under him, pinning him to the ground.

All the rebels are unconscious, many are bleeding, but no one's dead. The leader lifts his head and lets out a low moan. I look into his eyes and see something so familiar I almost lose my breath: His look is one of loss. His people have been defeated, just like mine were so long ago.

The desert dissolves around us. We're standing back in the station. The sim is over.

"Congratulations, Unit Fifteen," Magister Sethra says, smiling proudly. "If this had been the actual examination, you all would have passed. Excellent leadership, Cadet Li."

I hear her words, but I don't feel any relief. For the first time, what I'm doing becomes fully clear to me. I'm joining the same military that eliminated my entire species, the military that bombed my home planet, the one that killed my family. I wait to feel victorious. I wait to feel anything but this sinking in my stomach, until I feel nothing at all.

After Sethra dismisses us, I walk across the base, hoping to find some semblance of calm, a space where I can think. I stop at a narrow stretch of beach, wild and untamed. The trees reach out over the water, light glittering through their leaves.

I slip my feet out of my boots and bury my toes in the sand. The waves dissolve into foam as they reach the shore. I stare at the sand on the ocean floor, watching the delicate motion of each grain shifting. I led the unit safely, we completed our mission, but today's victory seems hollow and far away, like it doesn't even belong to me. It wasn't real, I tell myself, but I see my hands ripping the mask from the rebel's face. I feel her body shudder as she takes her last breath.

"Li!" a voice calls out, and I turn from the water to see Ryn walking toward me.

"I was hoping I'd find you," he says once he reaches me. "You raced out of there after the sim."

"It was harder than I thought it would be," I say, averting my eyes. "I feel like I don't know what I'm doing."

Ryn steps closer to me. "None of us knows what we're doing," he says gently. "We're all trying our hardest to pretend we do. Our lives are changing completely, and there's barely any time for us to catch up."

I stare at the waves crashing against the shore, the ocean endless before us. I think about what Zo said, wonder if it's true that I can't be happy for her. Abdoloreans believe humans were soulless somehow—what if they were right?

Ryn watches me. He takes my hand in his, a look of concern crossing his face.

"You're shaking," he says. "Are you okay?"

I pull my hand away.

"I'm fine," I say. "It's just . . ." I trail off, unsure of what to say next.

"Li," he says quietly, and I look up at him. "I know."

What do you know? I think, searching his eyes with my own. Ryn reaches up and touches my cheekbone.

"Your freckles, right here," he says softly. "They're like a constellation. You have your very own stars."

He runs his hands through my hair until he's holding my shoulders, pulling me toward him. My eyes flutter closed. I lift my face to his.

This is happening. And this time I don't stop it.

Ryn brushes his lips against my mine and the world opens, explodes. I kiss him back. I kiss him over and over. He pulls away, resting his forehead against mine.

"I've wanted to do that since the first day I saw you," he says, his voice low.

I'm afraid that if I speak, all my secrets will come tumbling out. Instead, I press my mouth to his, kissing him again, hoping he feels what I hold inside.

ten

I walk home in a daze, in another universe completely. I barely notice when I reach my street, my house. I press my hand up to my lips, feeling Ryn against me, his arms holding me as though nothing else matters. How is it possible to want something so badly, something you didn't even know existed before?

I pick a handful of berries from the bowl on the counter and head upstairs. The door to Zo's room is closed, but I hear the slight rustle of movement behind it. Whatever anger I felt toward her before is gone now. I just need to talk to my sister.

"Zo?" I call through the door. "Are you in there?"

I wait a few seconds, then press my hand to the door

and step into her room. She's lying on her bed, reading. She scans the pages quickly, barely looking up at me. I stand in the doorway, searching for something to say.

"What are you reading?" I ask.

"Advancement and Innovation in Environmental Preservation Technologies," she says, making a face.

She tosses the book down onto the bed and sighs, staring up at the ceiling.

"We haven't really talked all week," I say, walking into the room and sitting down at the foot of her bed.

Zo shrugs one shoulder in what I know is frustration. "That's what happens when you avoid someone," she says, and my cheeks burn.

"I know," I say. "I haven't been around."

Zo is quiet, staring down at her hands.

"I'm sorry," I say. "I'm here now."

"You said some pretty awful things about Braxon," she says. "And you know how I feel about him."

"You said some awful things about me," I reply, and she turns away, avoiding my eyes.

Zo isn't someone who moves on from a fight easily, but when she does, it's with her whole heart. Still, she won't look at me, and I stand up to leave, trying to find some way to make her let it all go.

"Come down to the water with me," I say. "Come swim."

A sliver of a smile appears on her lips, and soon we're

outside, walking down the cliff and onto the beach. We slip out of our clothes and walk into the water, wade in up to our knees, and dive under.

"Look up," Zo says when we surface, pointing to the sky. "It's a solar eclipse."

The shadow of the moon slips over the sun, making it a crescent in the sky. Golden light spills out around us, and the whole world glows.

"You know what this means," I say. "There's a new moon tonight."

Zo looks at me, but I can't see her expression in the growing darkness. I don't know what she's thinking.

"Remember our new moon rituals?" she asks quietly.

When we were younger and our father first taught us about the way the moon moves, the way it carries the tides with its gravity, how it sometimes covers the sun completely, we would send our wishes into the sky on the night of the new moon. This tradition became a part of the way we lived, a seam running through our months, our years, until we grew older and our attention moved on to other things. I wonder what Zo's life will be like once I'm gone, if the years we're apart will change us.

"Of course I remember," I say. I slip my hand into hers and look up at the sky. She follows my gaze, watching as the moon covers the sun completely and the world falls into darkness.

I feel the same rush I used to feel when we were kids, like we were part of the energies making the moon move, like we held the planets themselves in orbit and the world would give us anything we asked for.

Zo closes her eyes.

I ask for survival, I think, the same thing I've wished for my entire life.

We watch as the sun reappears, the world bathed once again in light. We don't talk, we don't move, we just stand in the water and stare up at the sky, thinking about what we want. I consider the dreams I hold deep inside, the ones I don't let anyone see, the ones I want most but never let myself ask for.

I ask for love. The words run through my mind over and over, and I feel like I'm filled with the moon and stars, with the sky itself.

Zo and I sit together at the edge of the water, watching as day fades into night. So much has happened these past few days; my world has changed completely. I lean my head against Zo's shoulder, happy to have her.

"Listen," I say to her. "About Braxon."

Zo tenses slightly.

"I'm sorry," I say. "I don't know him well enough to judge. If you like him, he must be okay."

"Do you mean that?" she asks warily.

"I do," I tell her truthfully.

She smiles, her blue eyes sparkling, her face flushed. "I really like him, Li."

She looks up at the sky. Her skin glows in the moonlight. She's spent her life in hiding, too. She's kept my secret for me, never knowing anything else. She deserves to be happy, to have the things she wants. We both do.

"The other day, you asked me about Ryn," I say, my heart beating faster as I say his name. "I didn't tell you the truth."

"What do you mean?" she asks.

The stars blink above us, and I imagine floating through them, close enough to feel their light on my skin.

"I'm falling for him," I say, my voice quiet.

Zo is still for a moment, then she breaks into a smile.

"I knew it!" she says, clapping her hands. "I knew you were into him."

She laughs and throws her arms around me, kissing me on the cheek.

"I wanted to tell you how I felt, before," I say.

Zo nods, understanding what I mean without me having to say anything more. "I've been sneaking out to see Braxon after you go to bed, or when you and Dad are training."

"Zo! Seriously?"

She looks at me, hurt. "I like him a lot. Try to understand."

She's right; I don't understand. But I look at my sister's hopeful face and I know I have to try. Her heart is so open. She sees the good in others; there must be good in Braxon, too.

"No more secrets," she says, her face growing serious.

"No more secrets," I promise.

The waves rush to shore, the sound filling the air around us. Zo leans her head against mine.

"I'll miss you," she says, so softly I barely hear her, and I know she's talking about Conscription, about the years to come.

"I'll miss you more," I say thickly.

When we finally go back upstairs and into the house, whatever distance there was between us has disappeared. I walk to my room and Zo walks to hers. Before she opens her door, she turns around.

"I'm really happy for you," she says.

Me too, I think, going into my room and lying down on the bed. I look at the skylight. The sliver of sky it captures is so familiar, the same moon and stars I've seen for the past sixteen years. I listen to the wind as it curves around the house, to all the sounds Earth makes. I breathe in and out, and the weight of everything I've been holding in begins to fall away.

eleven

The next week, I move through training as quickly as I can, running circles around the track, going through round after round of circuits. I sit through afternoons of lectures, learning about the resistance movements on Tevru and Velparian policies of engagement. All I want is to be alone with Ryn. Every time he looks at me, every time he smiles, I think of the way his mouth felt on mine and can't remember anything else. One hour slips into the next, each one dragging on, until each day is over. I wait for Ryn on the train platform, leaning back against a girder, looking up at the awnings, looking out over the crowd. The minutes pass slowly, stretching out before me. Finally, Ryn comes up beside me, kissing me on the cheek.

"You found me," I say, joy rushing through me.

"I could find you anywhere," he says.

The train moves across the ocean, winding along the edge of the base, pulling to a stop. We step inside and sit facing each other, our knees touching. I look out at the city in the distance, the way it sparkles, the way it shines, and I have the distinct sense of freedom, of light.

As we walk through the forest, Ryn asks me about the names of the flowers he sees. Thin streams of sunlight break through the trees, surrounding us both.

"What's that one?" he asks, pointing down to a plant. It has three leaves shaped like teardrops, a white line running down the middle of each leaf.

"Pipsissewa," I say.

"And that one?" He points to a flower with bright orange petals.

"Calendula," I say.

We reach my house and walk through the garden, picking fruit as we go. We sit on the cliff and eat the cherries we've gathered, their flesh dark and sweet.

"What did you eat on other planets?" I ask, holding the pit of a cherry between my teeth.

"It depended on the planet," he says. "Tularans are hunters, they eat mostly meat, so obviously I didn't eat that. The fruit there is completely different from what we grow here."

"How so?" I ask.

"There aren't many trees there," he says. "All their fruit grows underground, in these bogs at the base of the mountains."

We reach into the bowl at the same time, our fingers touching.

"They grow mostly berries, but they're not like the ones on Earth. They're not very good," he laughs.

I try to imagine his life there, how he spent his days, what stars he saw at night.

"Was there any part of living across the galaxy you didn't like?" I want to know everything about him, to know him completely.

"It was hard to make friends," he says. "I got used to being on my own. Most of the time, it was just me and my brother, and, well . . ." He trails off.

I reach for his hand, twining our fingers together.

"You're lucky, you know, to have the family that you do," he says. "Sometimes I get the feeling my parents can't wait for me to leave."

"Don't say that," I tell him, but he just shrugs.

"It's okay," he says. "I don't really want to be around them, either."

He stretches out in the grass, folding his arms behind his head. I lie down beside him, looking up at the sky.

"What will you miss most?" he asks.

"Zo," I say without hesitation.

"I love that about you," he says. "How close you are with your family."

He turns to face me. He trails his hand down the length of my arm.

"What about you?" I ask. "What will you miss?"

He moves closer until there's no space left between us. He kisses a line down my throat, the dip of my collarbone. I wrap my arms around him, pulling him over me. He slips his hand under my shirt, his fingers moving lightly over my skin. I close my eyes, I disappear completely, and then a shadow falls over us.

"What is this?" my father says, his voice dangerously quiet. I push Ryn off, panic flooding through me. Ryn stumbles to his feet, his cheeks flushing deeply. I push myself off the ground and look up at my father.

"Dad," I start, searching for the words to explain. "This—this is Ryn. He's in my unit."

"I don't care who he is," my father says, turning his glare to Ryn.

"Dad," I say, my voice rising, "please."

"Don't say another word, Li," he commands, and the look on his face is so serious, I fall silent at once.

Ryn looks at me, his eyes asking what to do.

"Go," I whisper to him. He turns to leave, glancing back, concerned, but there's nothing I can say to him now. I watch him walk away until I can't see him anymore, then force myself to look at my father, to meet his eyes with mine.

"How could you be so careless?" my father says, his words cutting through me.

"Dad," I say, my voice breaking. "I'm sorry. I didn't mean for you to find out this way."

It's as though he hasn't even heard me. He paces the length of the cliff, his eyes dark. "Do you even realize how dangerous it is to get involved with someone like him?" my father demands. He doesn't need to say it, I know what he means—someone like Ryn, so different from me, someone Abdolorean. "After everything I've taught you. After all your training, all your hard work. Are you *trying* to get yourself killed?"

My throat tightens. My voice falls to a whisper. "Of course not."

"You sure aren't acting like it," my father says sharply, and I flinch. "I want you to think, really think, about what it is you're doing," he goes on. "How much time do you expect to spend with this boy until he figures out just who you are?"

"He won't," I say weakly, staring out at the ocean. "No one else has."

He stares at me without saying a word, and I know I've already lost this fight.

"Everything we do is so you can live," he says. "So

you can survive. You're not going to throw that away over some stranger."

The look in his eyes is unforgiving. I stare down at his feet, his boots scuffed from years of wear.

"He's not a stranger," I whisper.

"Don't be foolish," he says harshly. "It's over now, do you understand me?"

I meet his gaze, my eyes already filled with tears.

"Answer me," he says. "Tell me you understand."

"Yes," I say past the lump in my throat. "I understand."

That night, I lie in bed, my heart aching in a way I've never felt before. The door to my room slides open. I half expect it to be my dad, here to apologize, but Zo climbs into bed next to me. I close my eyes, pretending to sleep.

"I know you're awake," she says, curling up against me. I can hear the happiness in her voice.

She pokes my rib cage, hard, until I turn over to face her.

"Braxon asked me to be his girlfriend," she whispers.

I don't say anything, thinking of Ryn, knowing if I speak I'll only start to cry. She keeps talking, and I try to listen. I try to be happy for her, but my mind is scattered, unfocused, darting between the past and now.

When we were younger, our father told us stories about the way life was on Earth during his first missions. Zo's favorite stories were about the houses humans lived in, houses made of wood, with doors that opened using keys, but my favorite story was always about fireflies.

Imagine, he would say, a creature that lit up like the stars to find its mate. He told us that the night sky was once filled with fireflies, that he would catch them in his hands, watching them glow, before releasing them back to the air. I liked to think of my own skin glowing, my body blinking in the darkness to find someone to love, someone who could love me back.

But when I close my eyes now, there is no flicker, no light.

Only darkness.

twelve

Throughout training the next day, I stand off to the side, avoiding the other cadets, avoiding Ryn. He beamed me this morning, but I ignored it, watching his outline flicker until it disappeared. I don't know what to say to him.

"To complete today's training, you are to run the perimeter of the base," Sethra says. "Once you've finished, you're free to spend the afternoon however you would like."

We line up in front of the station. Braxon and Akia take off together, Ranthu, Ryn, Nava, and Mirabae behind them. I start to run, slowly at first, then faster and faster, until I'm ahead of everyone else. We circle the base, running past the train tracks, under bridges. We go through the woods, darting around trees, leaping over stones, over streams. We're one long line of bodies, flying.

I hear the fall of footsteps behind me, someone coming closer. Ryn runs up beside me.

"Hey," he says, keeping pace with me.

"Hi," I say, and start to run faster.

"Are you okay?" he says. "I beamed you but you didn't answer."

I look at him, at the worry in his eyes. All I'm going to do is hurt him. I can't make this any harder than it already is.

"I can't talk about this right now," I say shortly, and break away from him. I don't look back, scared to see the expression on his face if I do.

I run until my mind goes blank. I run until I feel like my body will split apart. I think only of my feet hitting the ground, my arms pumping at my sides, all the life my body holds. I hear the blood rush through me, I feel my heart pound in my chest. I run until I can't go on, then drop down to the ground. The rest of the group soon follows, and we sit in a circle and catch our breath.

I stand up and stretch out my legs, my arms, pressing my hands flat to the ground. Ryn walks over to me.

"Can we talk?" he asks.

I hesitate, avoiding his eyes.

"Okay," I say. "But not here."

We walk past the station, toward the woods. Ryn takes my hand, squeezing it gently. My heart clenches in response. I wait until we reach a clearing in the trees to look him in the eyes.

"Ryn," I say, letting go of his hand. "I can't do this."

"What do you mean?" he asks, confused.

"This, whatever this is," I say, my breath catching in my throat.

We stand among the birch trees. Wildflowers bloom at our ankles. From the other side of base, the train rushes across the tracks, the ground shaking beneath us.

"Is this because of your dad?" he asks, his voice filled with concern. "I can come over and apologize. Once he gets to know—"

"No," I interrupt. "It's because of you."

Ryn's eyes darken with distress. "Li, I—"

I cut him off again. "We got carried away. What did you think was going to come of this, anyway?" My voice is colder than I've ever heard it before. "We're leaving in two months." I push down the despair I feel rising within me. There's no way for me to be with him and protect my family, myself. There's nothing left to do but end it.

"I thought about it. I can't be with you," I say. "I'm sorry."

Ryn flinches, pressing his lips together. For a moment, I think he's going to say something, but he just shakes his head and walks away. The way his body moves is something I know, something familiar to me now. I want to call his name and run to him, I want to take it all back. I close my eyes and press my palms against them. When I open them, he's gone. I walk back around to the front of the station. It takes everything in me to move forward, to put one foot in front of the other, as though I didn't just break my own heart.

Mirabae and Akia are the only ones still here, leaning up against the side of the station. Mirabae gives me a questioning look, but I shake my head slightly, my voice lost somewhere deep inside me.

"We're on our way to the presentation showing for the Planetary Orientation Series, if you want to come," Akia says.

All I want to do is collapse. I want to disappear.

"Sure," I say, forcing myself to smile. "Let's go."

We walk across base, into the auditorium. The room looks entirely different than it did on our first day. The ceiling sparkles, the image of a small silver planet projected onto it. Rows of seats rise up from the floor. Akia, Mirabae, and I sit down. As we do, our seats tilt back so we're staring up at the ceiling. The lights in the room flicker off and the planet grows brighter.

"Napru is the twelfth planet from the sun," a voice echoes through the room. "It's an urban planet with an electromagnetic force field that exists inches above its surface."

The buildings that cover the planet are tall and thin, each one made of solar paneling. They float just above the ground, suspended in the air.

"For generations, Napruans built their homes below the ground. Now all structures are built with material that holds the alternately charged force from the electromagnetic field."

The image before us shifts, showing someone walking down the street dressed in something that looks like a space suit, their feet hovering over the ground.

"Napruan outerwear consists of pressurized gravity-chambered suits that allow inhabitants to move around on the surface of the planet."

The presentation goes on to explain that Abdolorean technology is what made life aboveground possible for Napruans, that there are communities who still live belowground in resistance to Abdolorean presence, but more and more people are leaving for life on the surface. I can't stop myself from thinking that the Forces don't belong on Napru at all, that everyone there lived in a way that worked for them, one that Abdoloreans came in and changed.

After the presentation ends, Mirabae, Akia, and I walk to the train together. I know Mirabae can tell that something's wrong, but she doesn't ask me about it now. She'll beam me later tonight, and I'll tell her about Ryn then.

"My mother was part of the mission that moved Napruans to the surface," Akia says. "Back during her Conscription."

"That's incredible," Mirabae says. "Did she ever tell you what it was like?"

Akia nods. "She said that most of the older generation wanted to stay underground, but she worked with one woman who had always wanted to live on the surface, ever since she was young. My mom said that the first time they went up, the woman told her that being aboveground felt like learning how to fly."

I stare out across the ocean before us as we wait for the train. I look up to the sky, imagining myself high above Earth. I imagine myself flying, untethered from this planet, untethered from everything.

I've never felt so alone.

The door to my father's study is closed, the room quiet. I bring my hand up and open the door, peering through the darkness. I step inside and run my hands against the walls, searching for the spot that's hollow, where my father's safe is hidden. I find it easily, pressing my hands against it, hesitating only for a moment. I slide the panel out of the wall, revealing the safe. My father taught us the code in case of emergencies, and as I enter it, I feel a slight twinge that I'm doing something wrong. The safe unlocks. I settle down onto the floor, tucking my legs underneath me.

I reach inside the safe, feeling around until I find what I'm looking for. I open my hand and look at the ring in the middle of my palm. Even in the darkness, it shimmers, golden, the shape of a feather etched around it. The ring belonged to my human mother, her name written along the inside—*Augusta*. I don't know how to mourn someone I can't remember. Still, I wonder what our life was like together, before everything that happened here happened. I slip the ring over my finger, thinking back to when I was six years old, to the first time I understood completely who I was, what it really meant to be human.

My father and I were at the beach, searching for shells. We walked along the edge of the water, right where the waves met the sand. Seafoam gathered at our feet, dissolving around us as we moved.

"Do you think this is what walking on clouds feels like?" I asked.

"Yes, Li, I do," my father said.

I remember reaching down and picking up a peri-winkle shell, running my thumb over it, feeling the way it curved.

"Those shells have been here for thousands of years," my father said. "They existed before anyone lived on Earth at all."

He told me that the ocean was full of prehistoric crea-tures, sharp-toothed and monstrous, that the land was empty and untamed. I'd never thought before about how I got here, how anyone got to this Earth at all. My family came from Abdolora, but I was born on Earth, and for the first time, I wondered what that really meant.

"Dad," I said, and he looked down at me. "How did I get here, if I'm not like you?"

I was too young to realize that this was a difficult question, that it required him to be truthful in a way he hadn't yet had to be.

"I was wondering when you would ask that," he said, looking off into the distance. "You had a mother and a father who were human, like you," he says. "Your mother was named Augusta and your father was named Elia."

"Where are they now?" I asked.

"They died, my love," he said, his voice quiet. "All the humans who were here died, you know that."

"But not me," I said, and he took my hand.

"No, not you," he said. "Your mother and father, they

loved you so much. They knew what was going to happen to Earth, they knew their lives would end. They gave you to me so that you could survive."

He told me they were scientists, like him, that they spent their lives trying to save Earth. My human mother had brown skin and brown eyes, like mine. My human father was tall, his skin pale, his eyes a deep blue, like the ocean.

"They wanted the world for you," he told me. "That's why you're here."

I look down at Augusta's ring. A strange sense of loss rushes through me, resting just beneath my lungs. I have a father and a sister, I tell myself, alive, on this Earth. I have my family here.

The light turns on and I squint against its sudden brightness. Zo stands in front of me, framed by the doorway.

"What are you doing, sitting alone in the dark?" she asks. "Is everything okay?"

"Everything's fine," I say. "I just needed some time to think."

"I'll go," she says, turning to leave.

"No," I say. "Stay."

She looks at me, tilting her head.

"I don't really want to be alone right now," I say softly.

She sits down next to me, crossing her legs beneath her. She notices the ring on my finger.

"Your mother's," she says.

"I miss her. I didn't know her, but I miss her anyway."

"Same here," she says, her eyes quiet. "My own mother, I mean."

She smiles, looking down at her hands.

"I wish I could remember her," she says.

"Yes," I say. "I understand completely."

I slip the ring off my finger and put it back into the safe. Zo watches me, her eyes quiet.

"I broke up with Ryn," I tell her. "Dad found out about us, so there wasn't really any choice."

"Oh, Li," she says. "I'm so sorry."

I shrug, as though it doesn't matter, like I don't even care. I ignore the way my heart hitches in my chest, the way I can barely breathe.

"It's okay," I say. "It never could have lasted anyway."

We were going to end up apart all along, placed on opposite ends of the galaxy, away from each other for the next seven years. Still, we could have spent this time together, if only I weren't human, if only I didn't have to hide.

Zo lies on the floor, resting her feet against the wall. Her hair spills out around her. She closes her eyes and I watch her chest rise and fall as she breathes. She's the only one who really knows me, I realize. She's the other half of my life.

"Hey," she says, her eyes still closed. "Remember that game we used to play, the one Dad invented?"

"Which one?" I ask.

"The one with the electric rackets and glowing ball," she says.

"Sudden Death Turbo Ball," I say, the name coming back to me at once, even though it's been years since we played. "He used to get so mad at us for playing in the house."

She opens her eyes.

"He did. But whatever, he shouldn't have invented it if he didn't want us to play." She sits up, smiling brightly. "I found everything the other day. Want to play?"

"I don't really feel like it," I tell her.

She ignores my frown. "Come on," she says, jumping to her feet.

She grabs my hand, pulling me up and leading me into the kitchen. The rackets are on the table. Zo pulls the ball out from her pocket and tosses it to me.

"You have first throw," she says, taking a racket and swinging it lazily back and forth.

We walk out to the cliff and turn our rackets on. They buzz with electricity. The ball will never touch the racket itself. I feel the weight of the ball in my hand, then throw it into the air. It changes in color, from blue to red and back to blue. I swing my racket and the ball flies through the air. Zo hits it back to me, and I run toward it, reaching my arm out, feeling the satisfaction of my body moving, the way my heart pounds.

We play for hours, stopping only once the sun sets. We put the rackets back on the table. Zo leaves the ball on the counter, next to a bowl full of apples. I stare out the window, looking past my reflection in the glass.

The ocean is where it always is, the horizon even and unchanged.

Earth spins on.

I am still here.

thirteen

The next three weeks blur together, one day tumbling into the next. I wake up, I train, I come home alone. Every night, I dream of Ryn. I see him walking through crowded streets, his hair catching the light of the sun. I wake up reaching out for him. When I open my arms, there's nothing there.

One afternoon, I pass by the training compound just as Akia and Braxon go inside together, Braxon's hand resting on the small of Akia's back, guiding her through the door. The way he's touching her unsettles me. I hesitate for a moment, then follow them inside, slipping unnoticed into a corner of the room. The compound is filled with other cadets, everyone lifting weights, running, shooting.

I watch as they walk over to the climbing wall. Braxon

leans in close to her, whispering something in her ear. She tilts her head back and laughs, her eyes shining. She reaches up and puts her arms around his shoulders, lifting herself onto his back and wrapping her legs around his waist. He grabs onto the pegs and lifts himself off the ground, climbing the wall quickly, not faltering once, even with the weight of Akia's body on his. When he reaches the top, Akia lets go, flying down to the ground, a flash of silver in the air. Braxon leaps down after her, his arms spread out like wings.

Maybe it's nothing and he's just showing off, I think. Still, the sight of the two of them together, alone, unnerves me. I wonder if Zo knows. I wonder if she'd care. Braxon leads Akia over to the weight-lifting station at the far end of the room. I walk around the edge of the compound, keeping my eyes on them. Akia picks up an illuminated weighted disk and lifts it up above her head. Braxon comes up behind her and places his hands on her hips, spotting her as she raises and lowers the disk. After a few repetitions, she drops it to the floor. Braxon keeps his hands on her hips for another few seconds. My uneasiness grows deeper with every move he makes. Finally, he drops his hands and the two of them settle onto the floor to stretch out. I see their mouths moving, but I'm too far away to hear what they're saying.

I move across the room and slip into the seat of one of

the conditioning machines, my back to Akia and Braxon. They can't see me, but I can see their reflections in the metallic paneling that lines the wall.

Braxon jumps to his feet, reaching down and pulling Akia up. They face each other, holding their fists in the air.

"Imagine you're the enemy," Braxon says. "If I want to overpower you, I'd get you in a position where you couldn't hurt me, right?"

Akia nods, bouncing from one foot to the other, circling Braxon, just out of his reach.

"So either I'd get you on the ground, like this," he says, and swings a punch toward her. She ducks, closing her eyes, and Braxon sweeps his leg out under her legs, tripping her. She falls to the floor, landing hard on her knees. She jumps back up, putting her fists in front of her face once again.

"Or I'd want to get behind you and hold you, taking you out that way," he goes on. Akia lunges for him and he grabs her waist, spinning her around and wrapping his arms around her.

"Now, you try to take me out using the tactics I just showed you," he says, and lets go of her waist. Akia turns to face him, her cheeks flushed. She throws a few punches, but Braxon is quick on his feet, jumping out of the way.

"So," he says casually, blocking her half-hearted punches easily. "Are you with anyone?"

Akia smiles, dropping her fists to her sides.

"What's it to you?" she asks, her voice light, teasing. She darts toward him, fists up, but he catches her hands in his before she can land a punch.

"Are *you* with anyone?" she asks, and Braxon laughs.

"What's it to you?" he mimics.

They keep sparring, and I stand up and make my way toward the door. Braxon didn't lie to Akia about dating Zo, but he wasn't honest about it, either. I don't know whether I should tell Zo what I saw.

As I'm walking out the doors of the compound, Ryn walks in. He pauses, standing next to me. I study his profile in the light. *He's so beautiful*, I think, *and so far away from me now.* He turns to look at me. We're face to face; we can't avoid each other.

"Hey," he says coldly.

"Hi," I say. There's so much I could tell him, if only we were together, if only he were still mine. Before I can say anything, a shadow passes over his eyes, and he walks away.

I miss you, I think as he turns away.

"I miss you," I whisper, too quietly for him to hear.

After lunch, I get to the station just as Magister Sethra opens the door to let everyone inside. I step into line between Ranthu and Nava. I look at Ryn, taking in the broadness of his shoulders, but he doesn't look back.

"For your second practice simulation, you will be split into pairs," Magister Sethra tells us. "This mission depends on your ability to work together as a team."

A small part of me hopes I'll be with Ryn, but then she divides us up, pairing me with Braxon. *Perfect,* I think, my heart sinking. Braxon looks over at me, his jaw set. Sethra watches as we all move to stand together, waiting until we're side by side to continue explaining the sim.

"You will be placed in hostile enemy territory, tasked with collecting military intelligence. This is a reconnaissance mission. You must complete it as quickly as possible without being detected."

She doesn't explain the sim any further. She takes us to the back of the room, onto a panel set into the floor. The panel lowers until we're beneath the station in a room lined with glass booths. She leads each pair to a booth. Braxon and I step inside ours, the walls reflecting distorted slivers of our faces. We stand in silence, waiting. Without any warning, the lights turn off and the simulation begins.

At first it's so dark that I'm not sure where we are. Braxon and I are close together, our arms almost touching. A control panel ahead of me flashes on, filling the space with strange blue light, and I realize where we are. We're in a submarine, deep underwater. I slip into the seat facing the main control console, relegating Braxon to second-in-command. He gives me a look but doesn't say anything. I look down at the panel, surveying what's in front of me.

The screens are full of charts and lights. We had courses on navigational tools in school, but it's been years since I've studied them in detail. I struggle to think back, to remember what everything is for. The screen on the bottom is for depth and sonar, and those on top chart our course. The upper monitors blink rapidly, mapping out our path.

"You don't even know what we're looking for, do you?" Braxon mutters under his breath.

"We'll know it when we see it," I say, trying to sound more confident than I feel.

We sit in silence, pushing through the dark waters. I make a few tiny adjustments on the screens, but I feel useless. I don't know where we're heading or how far we should go.

"We should use our sonar, to get a better sense of our surroundings," I say finally.

"Bad idea," Braxon says. "If we do that, we'll reveal our presence. We're on a stealth mission, remember? Hostile enemy territory? Were you even listening to Sethra?"

His tone is harsh, but he's right. Of course the sonar would give us away. I should have thought of that myself.

Desperate to do anything at all, I turn on the manual piloting, hoping that by changing our course, I might see some hint as to why we're here and what we're looking for.

Kelp streams by the window, a bright electric green. We sink lower in the water, crossing over an abyss. This could be some kind of underwater cavern, I think, a place where the information we're seeking is hidden. I hesitate, then steer us deeper into the canyon. Rock formations loom on both sides of the windows, their shadows overwhelming.

"So," Braxon says, leaning back in his seat. "I'm seeing your sister tonight."

"Are you asking my permission?" I say. "Because Zo can do whatever she wants."

"Oh, I know," he says, and the way he says it makes my skin crawl.

"I saw you at the compound with Akia," I blurt out.

He stares at me, the flicker of recognition in his eyes so quick I almost miss it completely.

He shrugs. "All you saw was me training with another cadet."

"That's not all you were doing, and you know it," I say. "When I tell Zo—"

"Actually," Braxon says, cutting me off, "I don't think you're going to tell Zo. I don't think you want to have another fight over her being with me. We both know you'll lose again."

My throat tightens. I grip the controls so hard that my knuckles whiten. Zo told him about our fight? Braxon is the last person I want knowing anything about me. What was she thinking?

"She told you about that?" I ask.

"She's my girlfriend. Of course she told me," he says. "And I don't think you want to risk messing everything up just because of something you think you saw."

He's so smug, so sure he can get away with anything. I turn away, peering out the window at the darkness around us.

"Besides," Braxon says quietly, "even if you do tell her, what makes you think she'll believe you?"

I look over at him, not sure I've heard him correctly. In the shadowy light of the submarine, his eyes look sinister, unnerving. He leans closer to me, his knee brushing mine. I'm about to ask him what he means when the navigation screen begins blinking rapidly with bright white light.

"What's it say?" he asks, peering over my shoulder.

"We're in uncharted waters," I say. "We have to go back."

I've been so distracted that I haven't paid any attention to where we are. I peer through the window, seeing only the empty canyon. I look down at the navigation screen. It flickers once, twice, then goes dark. I stare down at it, trying to quiet the panic rushing through me.

"Our transmission is out," Braxon says, looking at the blank screen before him. "Our thermal imaging is shot."

He leans back and looks over at me.

"What now, Cadet?" he asks.

I take a breath, holding it deep in my lungs. I can't let Braxon see how nervous I am. My mind races through every action we could take. We can't release an emergency signal, for risk of being detected by the enemy. Maybe there's a way to redirect power, but we can't just sit here while we try.

I shift the controls in my hands, steering the ship up above the canyon, back in the direction we came from. Braxon moves beside me, flicking switches, trying to force a signal through.

From a distance, I see light flicker, so quick I almost miss it. I keep my eyes on the space the light came from, waiting to see if it flashes again. I don't notice the wall of the canyon jutting up before us, too steep to avoid, until it's too late.

I pull back on the controls, but I can't stop the ship. With a sickening jolt, we crash into the rocks. The ship rockets sideways and we sink to the ocean floor. Sand billows up around us, thick and black. The lights in the submarine cut out. I can't see the controls or my hands wrapped around them. I can't see anything at all.

The emergency lighting along the ceiling clicks on, casting our faces in a dim glow. A crack spreads over the front window, a spiderweb across the glass. The water will break through soon, trapping us inside, suffocating us. *This isn't real.* I breathe again and again, trying to slow the rapid beat of my heart. Braxon stares at me, anger radiating off him.

The submarine disappears; the ocean evaporates. The sim fades away.

"What did you do that for?" Braxon shouts, pushing open the door to the booth.

"Obviously I didn't mean to crash," I say sharply. "If you hadn't been distracting me, it never would have happened."

"Oh yeah?" Braxon sneers. "If you hadn't been such a complete—"

Magister Sethra cuts him off.

"Clearly, Cadets, your mission was compromised by your inability to work together," she says, her voice cold. "I expected better from both of you."

Braxon storms away, slamming his fist against the wall as he leaves. If he didn't hate me for calling him out on Akia, he certainly hates me now, I think, watching him walk out of station. Magister Sethra stands in front of me, her arms crossed over her chest, her expression unreadable.

"Cadet Li, come with me," she says. "There are some things I think we need to discuss."

Magister Sethra opens the door to her office and I sink into a chair, steeling myself to be reprimanded by the person I respect most. Sethra stays standing, her arms crossed over her chest, staring down at me.

"What happened back there, Li?" she asks, not unkindly.

"I don't know, Magister," I say, my voice shaking slightly. "We couldn't determine the goal of the mission. We didn't know what we were looking for. I thought I saw something in the water, but then I just lost control of the ship."

I don't tell her what happened before the crash, the casual way Braxon threatened me when I said I would tell my sister what I saw.

"Just because you've done well during Assessment so far doesn't mean you can relax your efforts," she says. "If today had been the actual examination, both you and Cadet Braxon would have failed. If today had been a mission, you would have died."

I stare at the floor, searching for the words to make

this right, finding none. I think back to the day I met Magister Sethra, my first year of school. It was the first time I'd been away from the safety of my family, out in the world on my own. I sat through her class trying to focus, to not let anyone see how scared I was. After the day ended, she took me aside. She gave me books to read and told me that she could tell how smart I was, how much success I would have as her student, if I was willing to work hard, if I could open my mind to learning all there was to know about the world. She was always proud of my commitment, my focus. Sitting before her now, I can't help but feel that I've disappointed her, that I've failed not just myself but her as well.

"I know how badly you want to make officer," she says. "I want that for you, too."

"Thank you, Magister," I say, hope rising quietly inside me.

The maps on the walls shift from one planet to the next, and stars glitter on the surface of the screens. I close my eyes, as though I can disappear.

Magister Sethra studies me, her face still.

"You've been distracted these past few weeks," she says, leaning back against her desk. "Is something going on?"

She waits for me to speak. I don't know what to tell her. I can't focus on anything. Everything feels like it's falling apart around me, the world dissolving completely. My heart is shattered into pieces in a way I don't know how to mend. My sister is falling for someone I can't stand, and all it does is remind me that I can't be with the one person on this planet I've ever wanted.

"I'm just . . . under a lot of pressure," I say.

Sethra murmurs in agreement, her eyes thoughtful.

"Leading troops is never easy," she says. "Being an officer means you have to make difficult decisions in an instant, decisions that don't have a clear right or wrong."

"How do you know what the right decisions are, then?" I ask. "How do you know you're doing the right thing?"

Sethra smiles, clasping her hands together.

"You're already thinking like an officer," she says. "There are no simple answers to those questions. You'll learn as time goes on how to trust yourself and your instincts."

I nod, even though I'm not sure I believe her.

"I really do want to make it," I say. "I'm sorry I let you down."

"This isn't about letting me down," Sethra says. "This is about what future you want to have."

She walks across the room and presses her hand to the door. I stand up and walk behind her.

"I promise I'll work harder, Magister," I say.

"I know you will, Li," Sethra says, and I step out of her office, the door sliding shut behind me.

As I walk home through the forest, Sethra's words run through my head. *This is about what future you want to have.* I run my hands along the leaves that line the path, remembering walking here with Ryn. I saw a future with Ryn then. When I close my eyes and feel the wind around me, I wonder if the future is something we can still share.

fourteen

I walk up to the house just as Zo slips through the door, holding her shoes in her hands.

"Where are you off to?" I ask.

"I'm meeting up with Braxon," she says. "He beamed me and said he had to see me."

She bends down, slipping her shoes on, her face flushed with excitement. I think about what happened during the sim, the cold way he looked at me, the sharp way he laughed. I remember the way he held Akia to him, like Zo didn't exist at all.

I open my mouth, about to tell her what I saw, when I notice the necklace she's wearing, a thin silver chain with a teardrop hanging down.

"Your necklace," I say. "Where did you get that?"

"Isn't it amazing?" Zo says. "Braxon gave it to me." Her cheeks flush and she bites her lip. "He told me he loves me."

She looks happier than I've ever seen her look. The words I was about to say stick in my throat. I don't want to hurt her; I don't want her to be angry with me.

"Are you in love with him, Zo?" I ask.

She runs her finger over the necklace, smiling to herself.

"I'm crazy in love with him," she says. "I've never felt this way before."

I force myself to smile. I force the image of Braxon and Akia out of my mind. Maybe what I saw at the compound was nothing, something I imagined.

"I'll be back later," she says. "If Dad asks, tell him I had to stay late at school."

I watch her walk away, ignoring the voice in my head, the one whispering that I'm lying to the person I love most in this universe.

That night, I meet Mirabae at the cliffs before the sun goes down. She beamed me, asking to see me, saying it was important, but she didn't tell me why she needed to meet so badly. I get to the cliffs before her, walking over to the edge and looking out at the world below. The city is so far away that the buildings seem miniature, like they're not even real. I lift my hand in the air, holding it over the shapes the buildings make. How strange it is, I think, to spend your whole life somewhere, only to leave, to go somewhere else, so far away from everything you've ever known.

Mirabae steps through the trees. The light her eyes usually hold is gone. She's wearing a pair of olive-green pants and a black shirt. Her hair is tangled, unwashed, her eyes bloodshot. She looks like she hasn't slept for days.

"Mir," I say. "What's going on? Is everything okay?"

She presses her lips together in a thin line, shaking her head.

"I need to talk to you about something," she says, unable to look at me.

"Mir, you can talk to me about anything," I say.

She stares at the ground, biting her lip. I reach up and tuck a purple strand of hair back behind her ear. She buries her face in her hands, and her shoulders shake as she starts to cry. I wrap my arms around her and she falls into me, like I'm the only thing keeping her standing.

"I don't think I can do this," she says, her voice muffled against my shoulder.

"Do what?" I ask. I take a step back so I can see her face.

"I don't think I can make squadron, Li," she says, pulling in deep breaths, trying to stop crying. "No matter how hard I train, I can't keep up. It's only going to get harder from here."

"Mir, it's okay," I say. "You're doing the best you can. All you can do is keep trying."

"I am trying," she says, frustration creeping into her voice. "And it's not working."

She sinks to the ground, resting her chin against the curve of her knees. All Mirabae has ever wanted is to be part of the Diplomacy Squadron, the faction of the Forces that travels from planet to planet, working with political councils to enforce Abdolorean policies. They rarely see combat, though they're called in as reserves when more soldiers are needed in combat, so they're not an option for me.

"I just . . . I don't know what I'll do if I don't make it," she says, her voice falling to a whisper. "I can't even imagine being in infantry, taking lives. Losing my own life. I don't want to die."

"Oh, Mir, I know exactly how you feel," I say, sitting down next to her. "I can't imagine doing that, either. I'm terrified I won't place as officer."

She wipes the tears from her face and smiles weakly.

"I didn't think anything scared you," she says.

I think about how far from the truth this is. The fear that runs through my life is constant.

"I'm scared all the time," I confess. "Especially now that Conscription is so close. I'm scared to leave home. I'm scared to leave my family behind for so long."

"I'm scared of taking someone's life," Mirabae says. "I'm scared of having to fight."

"You're getting so much better," I tell her. "I know you can't see it, but you are. You'll be ready to fight by the time Assessment is over."

Mirabae shakes her head. "I'm not so sure," she says. "I don't think I'll ever feel ready for that."

She looks down, her hair falling over her face.

"Mir, it's okay to feel that way," I say. "We all have fear and doubt, especially now. It just means that we're here on this Earth and we're alive."

My words settle around us, and I think of how my life has been split into two distinct sections. There's the part I can share with her, and then there's the part I share only with Zo and my father. My family will be safer once I'm gone, posted on some distant planet, where I won't be putting them at risk each day, where I'll live alone, without them.

"Li?" Mirabae's voice floats through the air. "Are you okay?"

I blink, forcing a smile.

"I'm okay," I say. "I just have a lot on my mind." I look at her, at her gray eyes, always shifting from dark to light. Something breaks away inside me, and I think, for a brief moment, of what it would feel like to say the words out loud.

"I know how you feel, Mir," I say carefully. "I really do."

The sun hits the surface of the water. The wind rushes past.

"No, you don't," she sighs. "There's no way you could ever understand. Everything comes so easy to you. You're at the top of our class, you're practically perfect at everything you do. Even if you don't make officer, you'll still place high in rank. I know you're trying to make me feel better, but there's no way you could ever understand what this feels like."

"You're wrong, Mir," I say. "This is so hard for me. Harder than you could ever imagine."

If there's anyone else on this Earth I could tell, it's her, I think, the skin on my arms prickling. We've been friends for half our lives. She's the person outside my family I'm closest to. There's solace in that kind of history, in the world we share. My heart pounds against my rib cage, like it could break me open. I pull in a shaky breath, aware that Mirabae's watching me, waiting for me to go on.

"The truth is that everything is hard for me," I say softly. "I'm not like you. I'm not like anyone else here."

She searches my face, her eyes unsure.

"What do you mean?" she asks.

This is a mistake, a voice inside me breathes, but the words are already rising within me. There's no stopping this now.

"Mirabae," I say, and her eyes meet mine. "Mir, I'm human."

Her eyes widen. Her jaw drops. She doesn't speak, she doesn't move, she doesn't do anything but stare at me in shock.

"Say something," I whisper. "Please."

"You're human?" she asks. I nod. "But . . . how?"

I take a deep breath and tell her about my human parents, about the way my father saved me. I tell her how hard I work to pass as Abdolorean, that no one knows but Zo, my father, and now her. I tell her how I could be killed, my family killed, too, if anyone ever found out. I tell her about my dad finding me with Ryn and the real reason I broke up with him. I tell her how lonely I am sometimes, that even Zo and my father can't understand. I tell her everything, and she listens quietly, without saying a word. She stares out at the ocean, the look on her face one I can't read.

"I can't believe this," she says finally. "I can't believe this!"

"I know it's a lot to take in," I say, swallowing hard. "Are you okay?"

Mirabae laughs joyfully. She throws her arms around me, holding me tight. "This is incredible! You have to tell me everything. There's so much I want to know."

I sink into her arms, her happiness contagious, my relief a world unto itself.

"Mir," I say, pulling away from her. "I need you to promise you won't tell anyone. It would be—" I break off, thinking of what would happen to my father and Zo. What would happen to me.

She nods. I search her eyes, finding only trust there.

"I won't tell anyone," she promises. "I swear on the moon and stars, on the universe itself."

She leans her head on my shoulder. I release a breath I didn't know I was holding. I could never have imagined she'd accept me this way.

"We're in this together," Mirabae says. "Always."

"We are in this together," I say. "And that's why I'm going to make sure you make squadron."

Mirabae lifts her head, a look of resolve crossing her face.

"You're going to make it, I know you are," I tell her. "We have a few weeks of training left, and I'm going to help you every day."

"Thank you," she says, her voice quiet.

"For what?" I ask, reaching for her hand.

"For everything," she says. "For telling me the truth."

The oceans shimmers before us, stretching out farther than we can see. We stand up and walk down the cliffs, our hands entwined, the world around us bright and new.

fifteen

Mirabae and I walk through the city, turning down the streets leading to the Emporium. This last week has been a blur: Mirabae and I train from dawn until after midnight, and each day she gets stronger, faster, more confident. Today I promised her I would go shopping with her, that we would find her a dress to wear to the gala. She's so excited about the night, she insisted on going now, even though the gala is still weeks away. For the first time, she feels like she has something to celebrate.

We walk in easy silence, the noise of the city surrounding us. My thoughts drift to Ryn. I wonder what he's doing now, where he is. I picture him as he was the first day we spent together, the way the light of the imaginary ocean made him seem like magic, like something I'd always wanted but didn't know until then. I look at the city around me, watching the way the sun reflects off the sides of the buildings. I wonder if he's thinking of me.

We walk down an empty street and Mirabae turns to me, a contemplative look on her face.

"What's it like, Li?" she asks. "To be . . . you, I mean."

I think for a moment, cataloging the way my body works, the things it can do, the things it can't.

"My body's more vulnerable than yours," I say. "I'm not as fast or as strong as you are."

Mirabae looks at me, her eyes moving down to my neck.

"Your gills," she says.

"Fake," I say. "My dad implanted them when I was a baby."

"Did it hurt?" she asks.

"I don't remember," I say. "I was too young."

She reaches her hand up, then pauses.

"Can I touch them?" she asks. I nod. Her fingers brush against the side of my neck and I shiver, even though it doesn't feel like anything at all.

"They don't feel any different from mine," she says, pressing her hands to her own gills.

"My dad designed them to be as realistic as possible,"

I say. "They're totally useless, though. I can't breathe underwater or anything like that."

Mirabae bites her lip, thinking.

"How did you do it all these years?" she asks. "How did you hide?"

I look up at the sun, squinting in the light.

"My dad started training me when I was really young," I say. "It was the only way I'd ever be able to pass."

I think back to those mornings, the way he pushed me so hard I felt like I'd never make it through.

"This is why you never come out, isn't it?" Mirabae says.

"Yes," I say. "There was always the danger that I'd be discovered."

"It was dangerous for us to be friends," she says.

"I don't think anything could have kept us apart," I say, remembering when we met, on the first day of school. We were eight years old. She came over and sat down beside me, her hair in braids hanging down to her waist. She told me her name, and I told her mine, and that was that.

The Emporium is shaped like a spiraling shell, its surface paneled with colored glass. We walk around the atrium, the air filled with arcs of color. We head into the bookstore, its walls lined with tall shelves reaching up to the ceiling. I wander through each aisle, pulling out a book of ancient Zatruan myths, another about the wild-life on Latni. I scan the pages, reading the first few sentences of each one, losing myself in the words.

Mirabae walks up to me, holding books of her own in her hands. We go to the counter and buy them, slipping them into our packs. We walk back into the atrium, its walls covered with ivy and wisteria. We each step into a chute and rise to the top floor.

The next store we go into is filled with clothes. Sparkling music floats through the air. Slips made of lace hang from the ceiling. Suits and gowns line the racks on the floor. I run my fingers along a row of dresses, some made of silk, others covered in jewels, all of them shimmering in the light.

"Li," Mirabae calls, and I look toward the back of the store. She stands in the doorway of the dressing room, wearing a long purple dress the same shade as her hair.

"What do you think?" she asks, and spins in place. The dress floats out around her. The mirror reflects her twirling, over and over, a hundred versions of her, incandescent.

"It's incredible," I say. "You look gorgeous."

She studies herself in the mirror, her eyes moving up the line of her body, until she catches my eye in the mirror.

"I'm getting it," she says happily.

She slips the dress over her head and pulls her clothes back on. We walk to the front of the store and Mirabae lays the dress down on the counter.

"How much is it?" she asks the woman at the register.

"Ten," the woman says, looking up from the shirts she's folding.

Mirabae reaches into her pocket and pulls out a handful of shells, counting them out on her palm. The woman wraps the dress in cloth and puts it into a bag. Mirabae hands the shells to her and takes the bag off the counter, slipping it onto her shoulder as we leave the store. We lean over the edge of a railing, watching people on the floors below go past.

"Hey, isn't that your dad?" Mirabae says, pointing across the atrium. I look down and see him, dressed in his lab coat, leaving the art supply store. We've barely talked in weeks, not since he forbade me to see Ryn. There's so much I want to say to him, if only I could find the words, if only I knew how.

"Li," she says quietly. "Go talk to him."

"I don't know what I would say," I tell her. "I don't think there's any way he'll ever understand."

"You have to tell him how you feel," she says. "Tell him the truth. All you can do is try. I'll beam you later."

I hug her and walk to a chute, moving down until I reach the first floor, following my father's movements with my eyes.

"Hey, Dad," I call out. He turns around, surprised.

"Li," he says. "Your sister asked me to pick up some paint."

He lifts the bag he's holding. People stream past us, going in and out of stores in an ordered kind of chaos.

"I'm heading back to the office," he says. "I have work to finish up."

"I'll walk with you," I tell him, knowing that if I don't say the words now, I never will.

We step out of the atrium, along the curving walkway that connects the city buildings. Before us, the ocean crashes into the cliffs. I take a deep breath and stare out at the horizon, gathering my courage around me.

"Dad," I say. "There's something I want to tell you, something I've been meaning to say for a while."

The hint of a smile crosses over his face. "I'll listen to whatever you want to tell me, no interruptions," he says.

The sun's light spills out around us, and I look at the ground, watching the way our shadows move.

"I know you're trying to keep me safe. I know that everything you've done is so I can live. But this, what I'm doing, this isn't a life. . . ." I trail off, trying to breathe, trying not to cry. Being human has never been so hard before, the weight of my secret pressing down on me in ways I didn't know it could. "You told me, the night before my exam, that I wouldn't just need to survive in this life, I'd need to live. I want a life, Dad. I want to be with Ryn."

"Li—" my father starts, but I cut him off.

"I can't ignore how I feel about him. I tried to, and it just didn't work. I need to see him again. I need you to trust me."

"I do trust you, but—"

"Dad," I interrupt again. "I'm leaving soon, and you can't protect me once I'm gone."

My father stops walking and looks down at me. "I know that," he says quietly.

I look at him, seeing the dark circles under his eyes, the way his beard is flecked with silver. I think about everything he's given me: a home, his love, my life.

"I know I can't stop you," he says. "If you're going to be with him, you have to promise me you'll be careful. Promise you'll stay safe."

I throw my arms around him, hugging him tightly.

"I promise," I say. "I promise."

I press my hand against the door to Ryn's house, my heart beating wildly. I wait for what feels like forever; then the door slides open and I look up at Ryn.

"Li," he says, his voice thick, like he's been sleeping. "What are you doing here?"

"I know this is crazy," I say. "I know that in a few weeks, we'll be far away from each other. I know that I'm the one who broke things off, I'm the one who said we couldn't be together. But all I do is think about you, all I do is want you."

Ryn leans against the doorframe, his face carefully blank.

"I miss you, Ryn," I whisper.

He doesn't say anything, but he doesn't walk away. He reaches out and pulls me to him, pressing his lips to mine, and then there are his hands, tangled in my hair, the broad expanse of his back that I wrap my arms around. There's the way his breath catches as he pulls away from my mouth, biting my lip softly. I let myself fall into him, let him hold me close.

"I thought I'd never get to kiss you again," he says quietly.

I kiss his hands, his neck. I kiss his chest, right over his heart. He takes my hand and leads me through the house, up a winding staircase into his room. One wall is made entirely of glass; the others have shelves from ceiling to floor. The shelves are filled with bird skulls and antlers, dried flowers and glass bottles, all the material artifacts of Ryn's life. I walk around the room, taking it all in, running my hands across everything he owns. There are small statues of mythical creatures, snakes with two heads, horses with wings.

"What's this?" I ask, pointing to a face hanging on the wall, its eyes half open, its mouth stitched closed.

"It's a Tularan death mask," Ryn says. "They bury their dead naked, wearing only the mask, to protect their souls from escaping in the afterworld."

He sits in the middle of his bed, his legs stretched out in front of him, his feet bare. The bed is messy, unmade, the sheets tangled. I walk across the room and sit down next to him, tucking my legs beneath me.

"Ryn," I say softly. "I'm so sorry about everything. I'm sorry about what I said. It was all so much at once, and I didn't know what to do."

He looks at me, his eyes quiet. I don't know what he's thinking. I can't tell how he feels.

"There are things about me," I say. "Parts of my history, of who I am, that make it hard to be close to someone. My father is strict, it's true. But there are reasons."

He looks up at me, his eyes as green as the hidden parts of the forest.

"Li, it's okay," he says. "None of that matters to me."

"It should matter," I say. "It does matter. You should know who I really am."

He pulls me toward him, taking my face in his hands.

"I know who you are, Li," he says. "I know that you're kind and beautiful, and when I'm with you, the universe makes sense. There's no part of you that could scare me away. There's nothing else I need to know."

I kiss him then, urgent, desperate. He presses against me. I fall back onto the bed and then he's over me, our bodies so close, moving as one. I feel the heat of his skin through his clothes, his heart beating against my mine. I think of the ways we hide from each other, and then I don't think about anything at all.

Ryn kisses down my neck; he kisses the space between my breasts. He runs his hands over the bones of my hips, holding on tightly, not letting go. I close my eyes. I gasp for breath, as though I have been underwater and I'm only now coming up for air.

sixteen

I walk through the doors of the compound and go over to the conditioning station. I step onto the running apparatus and set it to a steep incline. I make the first mile in just over six minutes, the next in five. I close my eyes and push myself to go faster, to move past the burn that spreads through my body. By the time I've finished the circuit, I'm completely out of breath. I step off the machine and stretch out, my body loose, blood pumping quickly through my veins.

Mirabae and I meet here every day now to train for a few hours before lectures start. We spend the mornings working out as hard as we can. We spend the afternoons learning everything there is to know about the other planets in the galaxy, all the facets of how the Forces operate, then go back to the compound to train more. I'm almost never home. I spend almost every night with Ryn, leaving his house late, walking through the empty streets, the moon lighting my way.

Mirabae enters the compound, her pack on one shoulder. She comes over to me and we walk to the weight station, grabbing crossbars from the rack. The crossbars don't weigh anything until they're activated, turning on only when they register the sensation of both hands wrapped around them. Mirabae and I face each other, holding our crossbars out in front of us. They flash twice with pale green light. Instantly, the crossbar holds fifty pounds. We squat, our knees bent, our backs straight, our arms shaking with exertion. We do a hundred repetitions and pause for breath; then we do a hundred more.

Mirabae lifts her crossbar above her head. She holds it there for a minute, for longer, then brings it back down. I copy her movements, mirroring the way she lifts her bar, the way she lunges. The lights on the crossbars flash from green to red, signaling the end of the workout. We drop them to the ground. Mirabae smiles, wiping the sweat from her forehead with the back of her hand.

"That felt really good," she says. "I feel like it's getting easier."

She rubs one shoulder, then the other. She tilts her

head from one side to the other, stretching out her neck, her back.

"You're definitely stronger than you were before," I tell her. "If we keep this up, you'll make squadron for sure."

We walk into the changing room, heading to an empty aisle in the back. I throw my pack onto one of the benches and take my boots off, listening as Mirabae talks about the gala, how she wants to spend the whole night dancing, then go to the bluffs and light a fire on the beach, staying awake until the sun rises. I pull my uniform off and go through my pack, finding my dress and slipping it over my head. I turn to Mirabae, tucking my hair over my shoulder.

"Are you still going with Cailei?" I ask, stepping back into my boots.

"Oh, that's so over," Mirabae says, pulling her shirt on.

"What happened?" I ask. "I thought you were into her."

"I was," Mirabae says. "But she wanted way too big a commitment. I mean, we're all leaving in a few weeks. It's not like she and I were going to spend the rest of our lives together or anything."

"You can come with me and Ryn if you want," I say.

Mirabae makes a face. "So I can watch the two of you make out all night long? No way."

"We're not going to make out all night long," I say, and she rolls her eyes. "Just most of the night."

We laugh and walk out of the compound, heading to the train platform.

"Love can wait," she says. "All I need is to make squadron, get placed on some amazing planet, and get out of here."

She talks about leaving as though it's easy, and I know that for her, it is. She's always wanted a life outside the one she has now, somewhere far away.

"Look, there's your boy," Mirabae says, motioning across the platform to Ryn. He walks over to us, lifting his hand in a wave. He gives Mirabae a hug and comes up next to me, kissing me on the cheek.

"Li!" a voice calls out. I look up to see Zo weaving her way through the crowd.

"What are you doing here?" I ask.

"Meeting Braxon," she says. She's wearing a jump-suit of mine, its fabric threaded with gold, and a pair of sandals that lace up her legs. Her hair is in a loose braid, flowers woven into it. She looks beautiful. She looks happy, like she's really in love.

"We've been together for two months," she says. "We're going out to celebrate."

She looks around the crowd, searching the platform for Braxon. He comes up behind her and lifts her in his arms, spinning her around in circles. Zo laughs wildly, wrapping her arms around his shoulders.

"We're going to the arcades," she says once he puts her back on the ground. "Come, all of you."

Mirabae shakes her head. "I can't," she says. "I told myself I'd read all of the squadron's material on code and conduct by tonight."

"What about you two?" Zo asks, leaning against Braxon's chest. Braxon puts his arms around her waist, his hands resting on her hips. I glance at Ryn, about to make up some excuse, invent some place we need to be, but he doesn't notice.

"I haven't seen the arcades yet," he says.

Braxon looks me over, his eyes a paler blue than I've seen before, like the open sky, like ice.

"Let's go!" Zo says, excited.

"Right," I say. "We'd love to."

We ride the train into the city, walking down street after street until we get to the pier. We go into the arcades, a relic from human times. All their old games are preserved, kept for Abdoloreans to play. Zo reaches for my hand and pulls me through the rows of consoles, stopping in front of a tiled floor, the squares of color flashing.

"Let's do this one," she says.

We jump from one tile to the next, music blaring, our

bodies lit up. Zo laughs wildly, spinning in circles, spinning me with her.

"Check this out," Braxon calls to us. He stands in front of a console, a gun in each hand. The screen before him shows a field filled with deer darting through the grass. He shoots them methodically, one by one, gaining points for each one he kills.

"Ryn, take a shot," says Braxon, holding out a gun. "Let's see who can hit more."

"I'm not really into that kind of thing," Ryn says.

Braxon rolls his eyes.

"Don't get all philosophical on me," he says. "Come on and shoot."

Ryn leans back against the wall, shaking his head slowly. Braxon looks over at me.

"What about you, Cadet?" he says. "Or are you like your boyfriend, who apparently doesn't know how to handle a gun?"

Ryn smiles, more to himself than to anyone else. He walks over to Braxon and takes a gun from his hand.

"First one to a hundred wins," he says, turning to the screen. He raises his gun and starts to shoot. Flashes of light explode on the field. One deer after another falls to the ground. He hits a hundred deer in under a minute, then drops the gun and walks up to me, shrugging casually.

"Not so bad for cruel, empty violence," he says, smiling.

"Not at all," I laugh, kissing him on the cheek.

We leave the arcades to explore the rest of the pier. We eat mangos cut into the shapes of flowers. We shoot lasers at glass bottles, watching as they shatter. We walk along the beach, jumping away from the waves.

"We should go to that new Kapnean place," says Braxon, brushing sand off his pants. "The one that serves those drinks made with flower nectar."

"I lived on Kapna for a while," Ryn says. "Those drinks are so good."

"So you'll come with us, then?" Zo says. "Braxon, tell them they have to come."

Braxon looks at us coolly, shrugging.

"Li and Ryn can do whatever they want," he says.

Ryn glances over at me, slipping his hand into mine. "We're going to head out," he says. "But you two have fun."

Zo unwraps her arms from Braxon's waist and pulls me into a hug.

"I'll see you at home," I tell her. "Don't stay out too late."

"We won't," she says, and smiles.

Ryn and I walk through the city to the train. We sit facing each other in the small compartment. Ryn reaches for my hand and brings it to his lips. A feeling I don't recognize rises inside me, at first nothing more than a whisper, blooming until it fills me completely. I close my eyes as the train races over the bridge and see us from above; I see us in the stars. We are here, together. We are everywhere.

Ryn beams me late that night, waking me from sleep.

"Are you busy?" he asks, his voice hushed.

"I was having a really great dream." I smile at him, pulling the sheets up around me.

He's standing by the door to his room, fully dressed.

"Are you going out?" I ask.

He smiles. "Yes," he says. "But only if you'll come meet me."

I sit up. "Where do you want to go?" I ask.

We decide to meet in the middle of the forest, halfway between our houses.

When I get there, Ryn emerges from the darkness. He comes up beside me, wrapping his arms around me, and I sink into him. I let him hold me tight. I press my lips against his neck, my heart beating fast.

"Li," he says, his voice low. "There's something I want to tell you."

He looks at me so intensely, I feel like he can see through me.

"I've never met anyone like you," he says. "Being with you has been so amazing, like nothing I've ever known before."

The branches of the trees reach out over us, swaying in the wind.

"I've lived all over the galaxy, and every planet I've been on, something's been missing, and I didn't know what it was until now."

He takes a deep breath, as though to steady himself, then he goes on.

"It's you, Li. I've been waiting my whole life for you."

"Ryn," I whisper, my voice caught in my throat.

"I'm in love with you," he says, and my heart flutters in my chest, so fiercely I could lift off Earth.

I look up to the sky, searching for the moon, the stars, something to give me the courage I need for what comes next. "There's something I want to tell you, too. But it might change how you feel about me, about us." My voice trembles as I speak. "I understand if you hate me for lying, or for what I'm about to say, but I need you to know. . . ."

I draw in a shaky breath, terrified to say the words out loud. Ryn looks at me, his eyes calm, and I feel the ground shift beneath me, the galaxy expand above.

"Li, I know," he says. "You're not Abdolorean. You're human, aren't you."

I stare at him in shock, in utter disbelief. The forest seems to condense around me, the thin lines of moonlight vibrating in the air.

"B-but . . . ?" I stutter. "How . . . ?"

He brings his hand up to my cheek, running his thumb along my jawline.

"The day we spent at the Cove," he says. "The way you swam, just a little differently from everyone else. Maybe it's because I've spent so much time on other planets, but I knew something was different about you. And then, when you got pulled under the waves, I knew for sure."

"You never said anything," I whisper. I can't believe that I was about to tell him my deepest secret and it's something he's known all along.

"I love you, Li," he says simply. "Nothing can change that."

Now that I've told Mirabae my secret, now that we're on the brink of the exam, I know what I'm doing is reckless. But because it was Mir, because it's Ryn, it doesn't feel that way.

It feels like what is supposed to happen. What must be said.

"It's true," I whisper. "I'm human."

Ryn shakes his head. "I don't care that you're human. I love you regardless. I love you because of it."

He lifts my face to his and kisses me. I pull away, resting my head on his chest.

"I love you," I say to him.

We walk through the forest, down my street, to my house. We go through the garden, the flowers around us fully in bloom. We stand by the door and stare at each other. Neither of us knows what to do next. I lean back against the side of the house. I reach up, running my fingers across the line of his collarbone, under the thin cloth of his shirt. His lips part and he laces his fingers through mine. I look up at the sky, watching the way the clouds move over the surface of the moon.

"How can we have so little time left?" I breathe, and Ryn pulls back, away from me. He looks down, kicking at the ground with the toe of his boots. He breathes in and lets it out slowly.

"I don't want to leave you," he says, his voice quiet.

Across the cliff, the moon reflects off the ocean and twinkles. I reach out and touch his wrist, his cheek.

"Who knows?" I say, pressing my mouth to his. "There's only so many planets out there. Maybe we'll be placed together. Maybe this doesn't have to be over."

Ryn keeps staring at the earth below his feet, as though he can find some answer there.

"I can't lose you again," he says, his voice a whisper. "Not when I just got you back."

While he looks at the ground, I look into the sky above. My heart pulses like the stars, entire galaxies exploding at once. I think of the way worlds are created in an instant, birthed from nothing more than the smallest spark in the sky. I'm still the only human left, the last girl on Earth, but I no longer feel alone.

seventeen

On the morning of our placement exam, I wake up before dawn, staring at the stars until they seem to move across the sky. I slip out of bed, wrapping the sheets around my shoulders. I walk to the window and press my hand against the glass. The window opens, revealing the ocean below. The waves glow as the moonlight hits them; they crest and fall over the shore. I breathe in, filling my lungs with the salt air of the ocean.

The sky turns pink, then blue. The stars fade, the sun rises, the night becomes only a memory. I turn from the window and walk to my closet. I take out my uniform, pulling it up over my legs, my hips, my arms. I tug my boots on, tying the laces tight. I braid my hair down the length of my back. I look at myself in the mirror, turning my body from one side to the other. This is the day my whole life has been leading to, what every hour in the forest with my father was for. I summon my courage. I reach for the strength I know I carry inside.

I walk through the hallway, passing Zo's room on my way downstairs. I stop at the doorway and peer in, looking at the paintings lining the walls. Some are images of her, one after the other, smaller and smaller, her body descending into the sea. Some are her face, covered in shadows, waxing and waning like the moon.

I look over at her, still sleeping, her body in the middle of the bed, her legs curved together, her hands tucked under her cheek.

Zo's eyes flutter open, as though she can feel me watching her.

"What's wrong?" she asks. She looks no different than she did when we were younger, her hair messy from sleep.

"Nothing," I say, crossing the room and sitting down next to her. "I'm just nervous."

Zo sits up, stretching her arms over her head.

"You'll ace this sim," she says. "You're so ready for it."

I shrug, not knowing how to explain that I could

never be ready for what comes next, for the possibility of failure, of discovery. Still, a sense of hope fills me, the feeling that I can rise to the challenge ahead.

"Li," she says, tugging the end of my braid gently. "You'll be okay."

"Are you sure about that?" I ask.

"Completely." She smiles. "You're incredible."

Mirabae, Ryn, and I ride the train to base together. I look out the window at the water below, listening as Ryn talks in a low voice, going over last-minute advice with Mirabae.

"The most important part of this exam is to stay on guard, to be aware," he says. "The magisters are looking at our ability to react quickly in a dangerous situation, so you want to be fully mindful of your surroundings at all times."

Mirabae nods, biting her lip, her eyes flickering with doubt.

"You got this, Mirabae." Ryn smiles. "You're going to dominate. Li and I will be with you the entire time. We'll all be looking out for one another."

The train pulls to a stop and we step out onto the platform. We walk through a line of arches that organize us by unit. The magisters lead us to a building on the far side of base, one I haven't seen before. The building is a massive dome, its surface mirrored, reflecting the sun's light, shining like it's a planet. The doors lift up and we walk inside. Magister Sethra stands before us, somehow imposing despite her small stature.

"For your final simulation examination, all units will be synced," she says. "You will all be in the same world, confronted with the same combat situation."

Mirabae glances at me. I slip my hand into hers and squeeze gently.

"Those named unit leader for this mission will see a star in front them," Magister Sethra says. I look around the crowd, watching as a glittering star appears in front of certain cadets. A star wavers in front of me. I reach my hand out, as though the star is real and I can feel it against my palm. Sethra's voice brings me out of myself, back into the room.

"Leaders, your task is to bring your unit safely through the mission, sacrificing as few lives as possible."

My mind races, going through everything we could be faced with.

"Cadets, on your marks," Sethra says, and we shift into position, standing with our feet together, our shoulders back, our arms at our sides. Sethra's eyes move down the lines.

"Begin," she says.

I close my eyes. The room goes dark, air rushes past, then I'm blinking in the harsh light of some unknown planet. The outline of the world we're in comes into focus. The ocean is gray, the sun almost blinding, the buildings burned out, deserted. I look at the abandoned city around us, struck by a sense of uneasy familiarity, like I'm remembering a dream. We're on Earth, I realize slowly. We're in the Bay. This must be a takeover by a foreign enemy, some kind of invasion. We're fighting to protect our home.

We stand in the middle of the street, in the shadow of a broken-down building. Shattered glass covers the ground. I crouch and open the pack I find by my feet. It's filled only with guns. I look up at my unit, from one face to the next, all of them with fear in their eyes. Even Ryn looks scared, and I've never seen him look that way before. My heart pounds, and I straighten my shoulders, take a deep breath, knowing exactly what we need to do.

"Listen up," I say. "We're too exposed out here. There's no way we can avoid an attack from this position. We have to get somewhere safe."

Akia looks past me, her eyes widening. A missile shrieks through the sky, spiraling in the air, pulsing with light.

"This way!" I scream. "Now!"

We run. The missile crashes into the street, right at

the spot where we were just standing. The pavement explodes behind us. Debris flies through the air. Nava turns back to look behind her. She stumbles and falls. Mirabae pauses, looking at me for some instruction.

"Mir," I say, "get everyone to the building over there."

I point down to the coastline, to the only building I can see that has any structure left. Mirabae nods firmly and runs ahead. I hear her voice carry, telling the unit where to go.

I circle back for Nava, pulling her up to standing, wrapping my arms around her shoulders.

"Are you hurt?" I ask, looking her over. Her uniform is torn at the knees, but nothing seems to be broken.

"I'm okay," she says, taking deep breaths.

"We have to keep going," I say. "We have to get to that building. Do you think you can make it?"

Nava nods shakily. We run down the street, toward the edge of where the city meets the sea. We turn into the building, through the empty space where the doors once were. I lean against the wall, trying to catch my breath. Nava slides to the floor next to me, her chest heaving.

The rest of the unit sit along the far wall. Ranthu holds his gun across his knees. Braxon and Ryn stand at the windows, surveying the perimeter. I catch Mirabae's eye and she gives me a nod.

Through a hole in the side of the building, I see

another unit racing down the street, dodging bullets, trying to find cover. I could call out to them, try to guide them to safety, but that would put our position at risk. I look out at them, my stomach twisting, trying to decide what to do. I can't save them, I tell myself. I can only save the people I'm with now. I move away from the wall and walk to the center of the room. I drop the pack to the floor and crouch beside it, opening it and handing a gun to everyone, keeping one for myself.

"What now?" Ranthu asks.

I can't see our enemies, but I know they're out there, hiding, waiting to attack. Fear wells up inside me. I have no time to think, no time to plan. I have to listen to my instincts, to what my body is telling me.

"We're going to defend our location," I say. "We're going to prepare for a fight. We'll each take a window and protect our ground."

Mirabae stands up and walks over to one of the windows. Ryn cocks his gun, the sound echoing sharply through the silence.

"Everyone, get in position," I command.

Akia hesitates, then walks across the room, crouching at a window and aiming her gun out at the street. Ranthu and Nava follow her. Braxon leans against the wall as though there's no danger, like we're not at war.

"Are you sure that's the best tactical decision, Leader?"

he asks. "I mean, what happens when the enemy gets here and sees us by the windows? This building offers us no protection. We're putting ourselves directly in their sight line."

I push down whatever doubt I feel and point my gun at an empty window.

"That's an order, Cadet Braxon," I say sharply, looking him straight in the eye.

He hesitates, just for a moment, then walks to a window, brushing against me as he passes.

I walk to a window and look out at the empty street before me. For a moment, the world is quiet. Then the shooting begins.

Bullets fly through the windows, ricocheting off the walls. They split apart and multiply, spinning through the air. From across the room, someone screams. I look up, the world moving in slow motion. There's Akia by one window, there's Nava, Ryn, and Ranthu. Braxon is bent down, loading his gun. And then I see Mirabae, a bullet wound over her heart, a look of wild desperation in her eyes.

She staggers away from the window and falls to the ground. Ryn runs across the room. He steps into her place, pressing himself against the wall and lifting his gun to shoot. A spray of bullets flies past him. He ducks, keeps shooting, stopping only to reload.

I crouch next to Mirabae, smoothing her hair off her forehead. She clutches her hands to her chest, blood seeping through her fingers. She stares at me, but her eyes are glassy, dazed. She pulls in one rasping breath after another, and I know it's the sound of her lungs filling with blood. There's nothing I can do to save her.

I look out across the Bay, at the murky water, the ashen sky. The streets in front of us are empty, but I see a flash of movement in the distance. The enemy's approaching, a faceless, helmeted throng of bodies. They seem to swell, to multiply, moving toward us at a brutal pace. If we don't leave now, we'll all be killed. "I'm sorry, Mir," I whisper, but she just gasps as the life leaves her body.

I stand up, wiping her blood from my hands, watching how the sun streams in through the window, covering her body, making it seem like she's made of light. Ryn watches me, holding his gun loosely in his hand. He nods briefly, the look in his eyes one of conviction, of resolve.

"Everyone, listen up," I say. "We're not safe here. More troops are on their way. I estimate they're about half a mile away, but they're moving fast. We need to get out of here, now."

"Where exactly do you expect us to go?" Braxon asks.

"Up," I say, and point to the sky.

We race into the hallway and up the stairs, flight after

flight of them, until we reach the top of the building, bursting through the door to the roof.

I look around at the nearby buildings, all too far to reach. I look at the city around us. I look out at the ocean beyond. I don't know if I made the right decision, leaving Mirabae behind, but I can't think about that now. It will be only a matter of seconds until the enemy arrives.

We stand above the water, the waves churning fiercely below us. For a sickening second, I remember that jump off the cliffs, so long ago now. I remember the impact of hitting the water, the way the water sucked me down, the way my body felt like it would split in two. I take a deep, shaky breath and push the memory away.

I turn back to my unit. Their faces are streaked with sweat and dirt, with blood. Akia is crying, shielding her eyes with her hands.

"We're going to die," she says, her voice panicked, her breath quick and uneven. "There's no way out. We're trapped."

"We're going to fail," Braxon says.

But Ryn is looking at me, his face calm, waiting for me to speak.

"We're not going to die," I say. "We're not going to fail. Not like this."

I look down at the ocean. There's nowhere else for us to go. Either we stay here and get captured or we jump down to the water below. I summon all the strength I have and step out onto the building's edge.

"On my count, we jump."

Ryn steps up next to me, his eyes clear and sure. Soon, the entire unit stands around me, balanced on the building's edge. I look at their faces. I look at the waves crashing below.

"One."

I breathe in.

"Two."

I breathe out.

"Three."

I leap off the building, I sail down through the air. I arrow my arms and legs, arching into a dive. The water is so far away, this fall so far down. I tighten my body against the wind, feeling my form lock into place.

My body cuts into the water, slicing in between the waves. I kick my legs, once, twice; then I'm above the surface, gasping. I count the heads around me, five of them in the water. We made it.

The world fades around us; the water disappears. The room lights up, and we gather together in an uneven line, disoriented, dazed. Ryn slips his hand into mine. Mirabae struggles to her feet, color returning to her cheeks, the wound on her chest healing before our eyes. It's over, I think, relief flooding through me. I stare at my hands as Mirabae's blood evaporates, leaving my skin smooth and dry.

Magister Sethra comes up to us, and we all stand at attention.

"Congratulations, Unit Fifteen," she says, smiling. "You have completed your final simulation examination. Excellent leadership, Cadet Li."

I hear her words, but I barely take them in. I watch as Mirabae runs out the door, her face buried in her hands, her hair streaming out behind her like a fallen star streaking across the sky.

eighteen

I follow her outside and into the harsh light of day. Mirabae stands by the door, falling into line with the rest of the unit as we pass. She moves uncertainly, her hand over her chest, touching her phantom wound.

"Are you okay?" I ask.

"I'm fine," she says, but she doesn't sound fine.

"What happened when you died?" Nava asks, her voice low.

Mirabae closes her eyes, tilting her head up to the sky.

"Everything went black and I couldn't move, no matter how hard I tried."

She takes a deep breath and her eyes flutter open.

"I knew in my head that it wasn't real, but it felt like it was. It felt like I died."

I glance over at her, but she avoids my eyes.

"You did a good job, Mir," Ryn says. "Really, you should be proud of yourself. You fought well and you died gracefully."

"I don't really want to talk about it," she says, and walks back into the auditorium, moving quickly through the room, weaving her way around other cadets. I follow her with my eyes until she turns and I lose her in the crowd.

"Should we go after her?" Ryn asks, concern crossing his face.

"No," I say, knowing this side of Mirabae well. "She wants to be alone."

We find seats and look out at the room. The walls are silver, the lights dimmed to blue. The crested wave of stars spans out before us, glittering in the air. As the auditorium fills, the magisters form a line before us. I go over the exam in my head, wondering if there was any way I could have saved Mirabae, if I could have made any alternate choices.

I did the best I could, I tell myself. There's nothing more I can do now.

Magister Sethra steps to the front of the room. She holds her hands out and the room quiets down, all of us anxious to hear how we've placed.

"This moment marks your true entrance into the Forces," she says. "This is when you all move forward into the promising lives you have ahead of you."

I clasp my hands together in my lap. Ryn looks at me, his eyes filled with trepidation. We both know what this means for me, for us.

The placement announcement begins, starting with the first unit. Name after name echoes through the auditorium, planets assigned, everyone's future decided at once.

Finally, they reach our unit. I take a breath and hold it. Akia, Ranthu, and Nava all place in infantry. Then, my name is called.

"Cadet Li, officer. Planet, Penthna."

I lean back in my seat and close my eyes. Relief washes over me, a wave so strong, so overwhelming, I feel like I could cry. Ryn takes my hand, leans in, and kisses me.

"You did it," he whispers. "You're safe."

We listen as his name is called, as he gets placed in squadron. My heart clenches, waiting to hear where. Ryn stares straight ahead, holding my hand tightly.

"Planet, Ursna," the voice echoes. All the hope leaves my body. My eyes fill with tears. I blink them back and stare at Ryn, his face mirroring my own. Braxon is placed in squadron, too, on the planet Senu.

The voice echoes out over us, calling Mirabae's name. I pray for squadron. I pray that all of her hard work these past few weeks has been worth it.

She ranks in infantry.

She's placed on Ativu, a snowy planet with a small

population. My heart breaks for her, as though it was my dream, too, that got so quickly crushed. She must be devastated. I look around the crowd, but I can't find her in the sea of other people.

After the announcement is over, Ryn and I walk across base to the platform, where the train is waiting to carry us home. One final announcement projects through the air.

"Congratulations to all of you, officers, squadron, and infantry alike. As you set out across the galaxy, never forget that you are doing your part to uphold peace and justice for all."

The words that would have once filled me with anger now only make me feel weary. Everyone around me cheers. No one notices that I don't join in. The doors of the train slide open and Ryn and I step inside, walking down the long aisles, passing Braxon as we go. He sits with his hands clenched into fists in his lap. He watches me, shaking his head slowly, his eyes cold. Ryn walks by him, settling into an empty seat in the back of the train. Before I can follow him, Braxon stands up, pulling himself to his full height.

"Looks like you got what you wanted," he says, just loud enough for only me to hear.

My body tenses. I try to walk around him, but he stays where he is, blocking the aisle.

"Don't do this, Braxon," I say.

He stares at me without blinking, then sits back down, his eyes following my path. Akia walks down the aisle, sitting next to him. She whispers something in his ear and he smiles at her, but still his eyes are on me.

I sink down next to Ryn, stretching my legs across his lap. He tips his head against the window and closes his eyes. The train moves over the bridge, away from the base. I feel the rush of motion, hear the rise and fall of voices around me. The tracks are a thin line over the ocean, and as we race across them, I look at the dark, quiet waters, trying to push down the distress I feel. The train picks up speed and the base fades in the distance, nothing but a blur on the horizon. Ryn rests his hands on my knees, and I remember the first day we met, at the Cove. I never could have known then all that he would bring me, the ways my life would change because of him.

The train pulls into city station. The doors slide open and we walk to where our families are waiting. I look across the platform, searching for my father and sister. Ryn kisses me goodbye and disappears into the crowd.

"There she is!" I hear Zo shout. She runs to me, her arms outstretched. She hugs me so hard I stumble back. Over her shoulder, I see my father walking toward us. I pull back from her and face him. I nod slowly. A smile spreads on his face. He steps forward and puts his hands on my shoulders.

"I'm so proud of you," he says. "Officer."

He folds me into his arms, and together we head home.

That night, Zo and I go swimming in the water below our house. We float on our backs, looking up at the stars, making slow circles with our arms, our legs.

"Are you ready?" she asks. "To leave the Bay, to go so far away for so long?"

I skim my hands across the surface of the ocean.

"I'm ready," I say, and find that it's true.

We stay in the water until our father calls us up for dinner. The three of us sit around the table, eating everything the garden has to offer, knowing that we won't be together again like this for a very long time. I'm quiet for most of the meal, watching my family, trying to hold on to the sound of Zo's laugh, the way my father's eyes shine when he smiles.

"To Li," says my father, lifting his glass. "For all you have accomplished."

"To Li," Zo echoes. She jumps up from her chair and runs into the kitchen.

"Where are you going?" I call after her.

"Stay there," she calls over her shoulder. "Close your eyes."

I put my hands over my face. I listen to her move around the kitchen, opening cabinets, slamming drawers, searching for something.

"Okay," she says. "Open them."

I pull my hands back and open my eyes. Zo stands in front of me, holding a plate of strawberries, each one with a flame sticking out.

"What is this?" I ask, confused.

"Candles!" she says. "They're called candles. I made them myself."

"What do they do?" I ask, watching as they flicker.

"Humans used them to celebrate important events. You make a wish and blow them out and then the wish comes true."

I close my eyes and lean over the plate. *I wish for my family to be happy and safe.*

I take a breath and blow. The candles flicker and the flames go out.

"You're sure this wish will come true?" I ask, looking up at Zo.

"Yes," she says, smoke curling through the air.

We pass the plate around, the strawberries the size of our palms. They're sweet and cold, and they stain the tips of our fingers red. For a moment, I forget everything that weighs on me. I can almost forget that at the end of this week, I'll be far away from everyone I've ever loved. All that matters is that I'm here with my family.

For a little longer, we're together on this Earth.

nineteen

I stand in my underwear in the middle of my room, waiting for Mirabae to come over. We were supposed to get ready for the gala together, but now she's not answering my beams.

"Beam Mirabae," I call out again. The outline of her body appears before me, shining silver. It flashes over and over, but she doesn't answer. I wait a few minutes then beam her again, but still she doesn't pick up.

She's ignoring me, I think uneasily. She must still be upset about not making squadron. The gala starts soon, though, and I haven't even started to get ready for the night. She'll meet us there, I tell myself hopefully. She just needs some time alone.

I walk to my closet and pull down the dress I'm going

to wear, holding it out in front of me. The dress is gold, cut low in the front and open in back. I pull it over my head and down my body. It falls past my ankles to the floor. I slip bracelets onto my wrists, their gemstones catching the light.

I look over at the pack in the corner of my room. In only two days, I'll get on an airship and fly to Penthna, far from everything I know. Penthna is all jungle, green and lush, filled with wild animals, and already I miss the ocean, with its salty, brackish water. I'll miss the sound the tide makes as it comes rushing in.

The door holo flashes. My pulse quickens, my heart soars. I walk downstairs and open the door. Ryn stands before me, dressed in black pants and a white shirt, the sleeves rolled up. He smiles at me, and it looks like he captured the moonlight and kept it all to himself. His eyes trace the length of my body, moving slowly up to my face. He meets my eyes, stepping closer to me.

"You're gorgeous," he says, kissing my cheek.

We walk inside the house. My father stands in the door to his study, and Zo sits on the base of the stairs. Ryn walks over to my father and shakes his hand. He goes to Zo and sits down beside her, tapping his knee against hers.

"I wish I could go with you," Zo sighs. "It's going to be so amazing."

"You'll go next year," Ryn says.

"Yeah, but it won't be the same," Zo says. "You'll all be gone and I'll have to go on my own, without my boyfriend."

"Something tells me you'll survive," Ryn laughs.

"Li," my father says. "Don't stay out too late. I want you home at midnight."

"How about I come back just after the sun rises? Or when the moon waxes high above the horizon?" I reply, smiling.

"I'm serious, Li," he says, but he smiles back.

"I'll be home by midnight," I tell him. "I promise."

I reach my hand to the door and press my palm to the glass. Ryn and I walk across the cliff, out into the world, the night unknown, still ours to hold.

The gala is held at the Celestial Plaza, a building made of glass with a winding staircase leading up to the doors. The walls inside are a deep blue, the ceiling covered with bulbs of light in the shape of the constellations. Music swells around us. The floor glows as we make our way across it. Ryn takes my hand and pulls me toward him, spinning me in circles, holding me close.

"I'm going to miss you so much," I say quietly.

Ryn closes his eyes, pressing his lips together.

"Let's not talk about leaving," he says. "Not tonight."

He leans down and kisses me softly.

"I'll wait forever for you," he whispers. For a moment, however brief, I believe in something like hope.

"Li, look," he says, dropping his hands from my waist and pointing to the door. "There's Mirabae."

I follow his gaze across the room. Mirabae storms through the crowd, her eyes unfocused, gleaming. She comes up to us, swaying slightly.

"Mir," I say. "What's going on?"

She looks at me, but it's as though she doesn't see me at all. I realize she's taken Kala and is in another world completely. I reach out to steady her. She shoves my hands away.

"It's all your fault," she says viciously. "Everything is a complete nightmare and it's all because of you."

"Mir, slow down," I say. "I have no idea what you're talking about."

She laughs sharply, her eyes dark with anger.

"The sim," she says. "If you hadn't left me there to die, I would have made squadron. If you hadn't been so selfish, if you'd had any idea how to lead a unit, I wouldn't be going off to some half-empty ice planet, waiting to be killed for real."

She stares at me, breathing hard. I take a step back from her, closer to Ryn.

"Mirabae, please," I say, my voice wavering. "How can you say that?"

"Say what?" she hisses. "That you ruined the rest of my life?"

I open my mouth and try to speak, but no words come out.

"You know that's not what happened," Ryn says to her. "Everyone was defending their own sector. You were shot. Li had to protect the rest of the unit. She did the right thing."

"Is that what you think?" Mirabae says. The strap of her purple dress slips off her shoulder. She doesn't bother to fix it.

Ryn looks at Mirabae calmly. He keeps his voice low and even. "You don't know that you would have placed into squadron even if you hadn't gotten hit during the sim," he says. "You can't blame Li for any of this."

"I do know," she says. "I talked to Sethra after we got our placements. I begged her to see if there was anything that could be done, but once the rankings are set, there's no changing them. She told me there was only one person ahead of me in the ranking for squadron. One person."

She moves closer to me, her expression shifting, her face dangerously calm.

"You wouldn't understand that, though, would you, Li?" she says softly. "You wouldn't know what it feels like to fail. You always get everything you want."

"You don't mean that," I whisper.

She arches her eyebrows and crosses her arms over her chest. She stares me down without blinking and my heart splits in two.

"I wanted you to make squadron," I say. "You're my best friend, Mir. I would never do anything to hurt you."

The music gets louder, the lights flash in slow motion. Around us, everyone jumps into the air, dancing wildly, as though nothing can keep them on this Earth.

Mirabae's face falls. I reach out for her hand. She pushes me away.

"I don't believe you," she hisses. "Human scum."

She turns around and runs off, shoving her way through the crowd. I watch as she stumbles out the doors, her hair gleaming in the moonlight.

I look at Ryn, who looks as shocked as I feel. He scans the people closest to us, trying to see if they're watching us, if they heard.

Mirabae's words repeat in my head, echoing through me, over and over.

"Li," he says. "Are you okay?"

"I'm fine," I say, but I feel my voice shake.

Ryn runs his hands through his hair. He bites his lip, looking at the doors, as though Mirabae could come back at any moment. Everything moves slowly, the world floating past.

"I think we should get out of here," he says.

We walk across the room, the floor glowing beneath our feet. We're almost to the doors when Braxon steps out in front of us.

"Leaving so soon?" he asks, looking me up and down. "You didn't even save me a dance."

"Back off, Braxon," Ryn says, his voice dangerously quiet.

"Yeah?" Braxon says, cocking his head. "Are you going to stop me?"

Ryn steps forward, his muscles tensed. I step between them, placing my hand on Ryn's chest.

"He's not worth it, Ryn," I say. "Let's go."

Ryn clenches his jaw, his fists, his whole body on edge. He puts his hand on my small of my back and I feel how it trembles. We walk out of the plaza, into the night. Braxon stands in the doorway, watching us go. The lights flash on, then off, and all I see is his outline in the darkness, a shadow, a ghost.

Ryn and I walk through the forest, the air heavy around us. I carry my shoes in my hands, my bare feet pressing into the dirt. I go over every moment of what happened at the gala. I hear Mirabae's voice in my head, her words cutting through me, over and over. Ryn stops walking. He reaches up and holds his hand to my cheek.

"It will all be okay," he says. "You'll talk to her tomorrow and everything will be fine."

I smile at him, but I truly don't know if things can be mended between Mirabae and me. Her words echo in my head, so full of hate, and I know something has changed.

"Let me walk you home?" he says, but I shake my head.

"I need to be alone right now," I say, lifting myself up on my toes to kiss him.

I start walking toward home, then stop, realizing I don't want to be there, not yet. I turn around and walk back through the forest, heading to the cliffs, the only place I can think to go where I can clear my mind.

I walk up the cliffs, stepping through the trees. I sit on the ground, dropping my shoes down beside me, tucking my dress around my knees. I think about the years Mirabae and I spent here, starting when we were eleven, just old enough to be out on our own. We spent hours here, entire days at a time, picking flowers and collecting stones, the world magical, ours to share.

Maybe she's right, I think. Maybe this is all my fault. I should have tried harder to save her. Her despair presses down on me, so thick I can barely breathe.

Behind me, the leaves rustle, and I stand up, my heart swelling, sure that Mirabae is about to step through the trees. The figure in front of me is a shadow, covered in darkness, and then it steps into the light.

Braxon stares down at me, his eyes glittering. His shirt is unbuttoned halfway down his chest, untucked and wrinkled.

"Waiting for someone?" he asks.

"B-Braxon," I stutter. "No, I just . . . I didn't expect to see you here."

He takes a step forward. I take a step back.

"Look," I say. "I'm sorry you didn't make officer. I know you must be really disappointed."

He laughs under his breath.

"You're sorry, are you?" he says quietly. Fog rolls off the water below, curling around us like smoke.

"Yes," I say. "I am."

"You know what, Li?" he says. "I don't think you are sorry. I think you failed our practice sim on purpose so I couldn't get ahead. I think you did everything you could to make sure you got officer instead of me."

He steps forward and grabs my wrists, bending them back. My bracelets dig into my skin and I cry out.

"Let go of me, Braxon," I hiss, trying to keep my voice calm, but he just holds me tighter.

"You think you're so much better than everyone," he sneers. "You think you're so much better than me. But you know what? You're not."

He pulls me forward, crushing his body against mine.

"Braxon, stop," I say, panic rising within me in waves.

He grabs my jaw, shoving his mouth over mine. His teeth catch my lip, drawing blood. He shoves me to the ground, tearing at my dress. I twist away, but he catches my waist and drags me back to him, pushing himself over me, twisting my arms above my head. I lunge up, trying to escape, then he wraps his hands around my neck.

His eyes flicker with hatred, sharp and pure. He leans over me, pressing his thumbs into the hollow of my throat. He brings his face close to mine and whispers in my ear.

"I know what you've been hiding," he breathes. "I know exactly what you are."

Cold, hard fear runs through my body. I stare up at him, my blood pushing its way roughly through my veins. He runs his hand down my cheek, down my neck.

"You should really tell your best friend not to shout out other people's secrets."

I rear my head off the ground and slam it against his. I hear the bones in his nose break, I feel them crack against mine. He brings his hands up to his face, wiping away the blood that drips into his mouth.

"You dirty human," he spits. "You thought you could beat me."

He grabs my shoulders and slams me down. My neck snaps back; my skull smacks against the ground.

"Braxon, no, please," I beg, but he doesn't stop.

"You're nothing," he hisses, slamming my head back again. "You're worse than nothing. I'll tell everyone and you'll be killed, just like the rest of your species."

He wraps his hands around my neck and presses down, his fingers digging into my skin. My whole body thrashes, my arms flail against the ground. Panic buzzes in my brain, a low, frantic hum. He's going to kill me, I think. This, right here, is how I'm going to die.

I reach out behind me, my hand closing on something solid, a branch fallen from the trees. I grab it and lift it high above Braxon's head, smashing it across his neck. I hit him again and the wood splinters. A shard slices into his neck, piercing his throat. He pulls in a rasping breath, his eyes blank, blood rattling in his lungs. He collapses onto me. He doesn't move. He doesn't breathe.

He's dead.

twenty

I crawl out from under Braxon's body and push myself to my feet. I look at him, lying in the dirt. I look down at what I've done.

No, I think, my heart pounding in my chest. *This can't be happening.*

I lower my fingers to his wrist, checking for a pulse, for any sign of life, but his heart has stopped beating. Already his skin is tinged blue, already the blood has stopped pumping through his veins. His eyes are open, clouded over, staring up at me accusingly. I slide my fingers over his eyelids, pulling them closed.

I have to do something, I think frantically. I can't leave him here like this. I bend down and wrap my hands around his wrists. I drag him across the ground, over to the edge of the cliff. His arms are stiff, his body heavy. A long line of blood seeps out behind us. I don't stop, I don't think, I barely even breathe.

I lift his body up to mine, holding him to my chest. These must be someone else's arms around him, someone else's hands. This must be someone other than me.

The moon is full in the sky, and its light spills over us. The only sound is the crashing waves, the echo of my ragged breath. I heave Braxon's body off the cliff and watch as he flies through the air. He sinks into the water, his arms floating above his head, as though he's waving goodbye.

I collapse onto the ground, digging my fingers into the dirt. I look up at the sky, the weight of what I've done settling around me. I listen for the sound of another person approaching, but all I hear is silence ringing in my ears.

Someone could come by at any moment, Ryn or Mirabae or anyone else, and I have no way to explain why I'm covered in blood, why I'm shaking so fiercely. I have to get out of here, now. I pick up the branch and throw it into the water. I smooth out the tracks in the dirt until Braxon's blood disappears, until it looks like no one was here at all.

I hold up my dress and run down the cliffs, my heart racing fiercely. The waves crash over the shore, the tide rushing relentlessly in. I don't stop running until I'm home. I climb the stairs slowly, careful not to make any sound at all. I go into my room. Zo is asleep in my bed, her back to me. She stirs when I come in but she doesn't wake up. I stand at the window, staring past my reflection, so I don't have to look myself in the eye.

I pull off my dress, shoving it into the back of a drawer. I bathe, washing the dirt and blood away. I'm still shaking when I climb into bed next to Zo. She turns over, waking up slowly, rubbing her hands across her eyes.

"Li," she says sleepily. "Where have you been?"

"With Ryn," I say. "At the gala."

She pushes herself up on her elbows, staring at me through the dark.

"The gala was over hours ago," she says. "I was waiting for you to come home."

I stare at the ceiling. Her voice sounds far away and strange.

"We walked around the city after, to have some time to say goodbye."

She studies me, saying nothing. I turn away from her, willing myself to stay still. She settles back into bed, falling asleep easily. I turn over and watch her face in the moonlight. The numbness that surrounds me splits open and panic sets in. If she knew the truth about what I did, what would she think? What would she do?

What will I do?

I wake up at dawn and get dressed, then head down to the water, standing at the edge of the shore, letting the waves rush over my feet. The world around me feels blurred, like I'm seeing everything through glass. I feel Braxon on me, even now. I see us drifting out to sea, forever bound. I see his face, his leering smile, his eyes glaring down at me, realizing just who I am.

I hear the fall of footsteps behind me; I feel the sharp prickle on my skin of someone coming closer. I turn, ready to see him, a corpse rising, but it's only Zo, coming up beside me.

"What are you doing up so early?" I ask. She rubs her hands across her face, yawning.

"Braxon's parents beamed," she said. "He never came home last night. They don't know where he is."

"They don't?" I ask, my voice hushed.

"Nope," Zo says. "They wanted to know if I had any idea where he was."

"What did you tell them?" I ask.

She looks out at the water and shrugs. "I told them to ask Akia," she says. "She's certainly seen more of him in the past few days than I have."

I stare at her. "What do you mean?"

She sighs shakily, trying to hold back tears.

"I went over to his place to surprise him before the gala. When I got there, Akia was there with him."

She twists her hair up off her neck, knotting it on top of her head. She wears a pair of our father's boots, unlaced, and a shirt that hangs down past her knees.

"I'm sorry, Zo," I say.

"You were right about him all along," she says softly. "I'm sorry I didn't listen."

My hands begin to shake. I shove them into my pockets so Zo can't see. She has no idea what I've lied about, I think. She has no idea what I've done.

Zo walks away from the water and sits down on one of the rocks that line the shore. I sit next to her, our bodies close together. She doesn't look up, but she leans against me, resting her head on my shoulder. The gala flashes in my head, one image pushing up against the next. I see myself in the mirror. I feel Ryn's mouth on mine. I watch as Mirabae reveals who I am, as Braxon takes his last breath, the light fading from his eyes.

Sooner or later, she'll find out what you've done, his voice hisses in my ear. I stare out at the sea, looking for some sign of him, but all I see are shadows, moving over the waves. There's no blood, no body, there's nothing there at all.

"Still, it's weird though, isn't it?" Zo says.

"What's weird?" I ask.

"Braxon," she says. "He's just . . . gone."

The wind picks up, rushing in my ears. A shiver runs down my spine, a deep, hard chill. How long can I hold this horrible truth inside me before I break apart completely?

That night, I lie awake in bed, thinking about the things that are my fault. I let my best friend die during the sim. I didn't even try to save her. I just stood there and watched her die, as though her life didn't matter. *It was all pretend,* I tell myself. *It didn't really happen.* But I know what was real—the moment I took Braxon's life. I've proven every Abdolorean right about the violence humans hold inside.

Ryn's outline flashes before me, blinking in the air. I know he's worried, but I can't bring myself to answer. He beams three, four times in a row, and each time I ignore it. Maybe he thought he could accept who I was, but he could never want me now, not after what I've done.

twenty-one

I float through the ocean, my dress gold, my feet bare. Hands rise above the surface of the water. Braxon floats before me, his lips covered in blood, his eyes empty sockets. I look into them, seeing only darkness. *You thought you could hide it,* he hisses. He wraps his hands around my neck. He wraps his arms around me, dragging me below the waves.

I wake up gasping for air, gripping the sides of the bed. It takes a moment for me to realize that I'm in my room, that I was only dreaming. I look up at the sky, trying to catch my breath. The sheets fall to the floor as I swing my legs over the side of the bed. I step over them and walk to the closet. I reach for a pair of pants and a shirt, pulling them on. The shirt hangs loosely off me, its fabric soft and sheer. I slip my hands into my pockets, feeling something brush against my fingers. It's the flower Ryn gave me, its petals wilted and bruised. My heart stills and I wrap my hands around it, as though it can take me back to the day we spent together in the curve of that tree, before everything fell apart around me. I let the flower drop to the floor, one more thing I need to let go of.

I walk downstairs and sit down on the couch, reaching for one of the books stacked on the side table. I swipe my finger across it. Words fill the page. It's a book of old stories, written by humans who existed long ago. I read about tiny winged creatures who lived inside flowers. I read about giant serpents beneath the sea, their scales luminous, their teeth sharp and lethal.

Zo comes downstairs and settles into a chair by the window. She opens her sketchbook and looks out over the cliff, drawing whatever it is she sees. Soon after, my father comes down from his room. He goes into the kitchen and I listen to the sounds of glasses clinking, of a knife cutting into fruit. He walks into the living room, his hands full. He sets bowls of sliced apples and blackberries down on the table. I reach for a bowl, holding it in my lap. The apple is tart and crisp, the sun streams in through the windows, and for a moment I feel like maybe this will all be okay somehow.

The Agency symbol appears in the air before us, a shark fin rising from the waves. It flickers for a moment, then fades, and a man's solemn face appears. His eyes are green, but for some reason they remind me of flames. His jaw is sharp, his dark hair slicked back. He looks out across the room as though he can see us, as though he's really here.

"Good morning, citizens of the Bay," he says. "I'm Chief Hael from the Internal Investigations Unit. As the lead investigator in the case of Cadet Braxon's disappearance, it's my duty to inform you that this morning, we discovered his body washed up on shore. We believe that he was murdered."

Zo gasps. Time slows, then stops completely. I look out the window, past the cliff, down to the ocean below. I think of what it holds, sand and water, empty space and all my secrets.

"May his spirit reach the stars," Chief Hael says; then his face disappears.

At dusk that night, we gather in the graveyard around the space where Braxon's body will be buried. There are lanterns strung along the cemetery gate, flames burning inside them. They'll stay lit for the next seven days, marking the time it will take for Braxon's spirit to leave his body and ascend into the galaxy. On the morning of the seventh day, Braxon's mother and father will come to the graveyard and blow out the fire inside the lanterns. His mother will leave her hair unbrushed and his father will leave his beard unshaven, so the world knows they lost their child.

We're all dressed in white, all standing, as is Abdolorean tradition. Braxon, too, is shrouded in white, his body cocooned, his face covered completely. A wreath of flowers rests on his head. The hole in the ground where his body will lie is dug straight down into the earth. He will be buried standing, as we all one day will be, as though prepared for battle. Even in death, he'll be ready to fight.

It seems like the whole Bay is here, whether to gawk or mourn, I don't know. I look around for Ryn, but the crowd is too big for me to find him. The faintest sense of relief runs through me. I breathe in, turning my eyes to the ground. There's a low hum in the crowd, a thousand voices whispering at once.

"It must have been a foreign attack," says the woman standing behind me. "It could have been the rebels from Tevru, or the gangs from Hulna."

Braxon's parents step forward. Behind them, standing to the side, is Chief Hael, his arms crossed over his chest, his eyes scanning the crowd. His uniform is gray, like the ocean at dawn. He catches my eye and an anxious charge rushes through me. I look away, staring at Braxon's parents.

"Our son was a kind, openhearted person," Braxon's mother says, her voice shaking. "He was smart and giving."

I close my eyes, thinking of Braxon's violence, his cruelty. But to his mother, perhaps he was kind. To his mother, he was good. We all live so many lives at once.

"All he wanted was to join the Forces, to protect the galaxy and bring harmony to the universe. That dream is gone, his life cut short."

His father points to the sky. We all look up, watching as the sun slips away, as the moon appears.

"And now," his parents say together, "from Abdolora to Earth, from first breath to last, we bury our son."

Braxon's body is lowered into the earth. His parents lay flower petals around the grave, to circle him with beauty and life. They gather dirt in their hands, throwing it into the grave. One by one, everyone around me reaches down to the ground. We will bury him together, covering him with earth, sending his spirit to the stars.

I look up to see Mirabae standing across from me. She meets my eyes, then turns away, slipping through the crowd. I tell Zo I'll catch up with her later and follow Mirabae, walking quickly through the streets to catch her.

"Mir, we need to talk," I say once I reach her.

"About what?" she asks, still walking, moving quickly away from me.

"You know what."

She stops walking and turns to me, but she won't meet my eyes.

"There's really nothing for us to talk about," she says. "At the end of this week, you'll be on Penthna, and I'll be on Senu, and none of this will matter anymore."

I stare at her, confused. "You were placed on Ativu."

She shifts from one foot to the other, still avoiding my gaze.

"Didn't you hear?" she says. "Since Braxon's position . . . opened up, everyone shifted up a spot in ranking. It turns out I'll be in squadron after all."

The street we stand on is empty, and I wonder what we look like from far away, two old friends, saying goodbye.

"Senu," I say quietly. "At least you'll be closer to the sun."

She sighs, running her hands through her hair, the way she does when she's nervous.

"I'm sorry I said those things about you," she says, her voice pleading. "It was the Kala. I know that doesn't change anything, but, Li, if I could take it back, I would. I was just so angry, and you were there, and . . ." She trails off. "I'm not going to tell anyone about who you are, I promise."

I look into her eyes, and I know I can believe her, because some things are unbreakable, still.

"I never should have told you," I say. "I never should have made you hold my secret for me."

"Don't you get it?" she whispers. "You should have told me sooner."

We're quiet then, the air rushing past us the only sound.

"I'm not sure I ever really knew you," she says. "I'm not sure what parts were really you."

"It was always really me," I say.

She just shakes her head, her eyes filling with tears.

"You're never coming back here, are you?" I ask, my voice breaking.

"Never," Mirabae whispers, looking up at the sky.

I take her hand, holding on to her one last time, and then she turns and walks away.

twenty-two

The next morning, I'm upstairs when the doorbell rings. A voice I don't recognize echoes through the house. I walk downstairs, into the living room. The door to the house is open, my father's back to me. I look past him to the person standing in the doorway, registering the gray of his uniform, the gun in a holster on his hip.

Chief Hael.

Zo walks in from the kitchen, scanning through the pages of a book. She looks up, startled, her lips pressed together in a tight, anxious line. We've prepared for this day—when the agents might show up—so many times, but now that it's really happening, it feels surreal.

"What's this about?" our father asks, raising himself to his full height.

"I have some questions for your daughters," Chief Hael says. "We understand that they both knew Cadet Braxon quite well."

"Yes, they knew him. 'Quite well' might be an overstatement, however." My father turns to Zo and me, and I know he's asking himself what the right decision is. Going through everything that could go wrong, every way I could be discovered.

"We can answer your questions," Zo says, her voice calm. "We have nothing to hide."

Chief Hael steps into the house, his eyes moving over the bookshelves in the living room, the walls lined with Zo's paintings, as though there's some secret we're keeping there.

"I'd like to speak to them alone," he says, his gaze shifting back to my father.

Dad hesitates, then nods and goes into his study, closing the door behind him. Zo sits down on the couch. Chief Hael walks into the kitchen and pulls a chair out from the table. He sits down, motioning for me to do the same. I sit on the edge of my chair, my back straight, my arms folded.

I remind myself to breathe, remembering everything my father taught me. I picture the nights we spent in the cabin deep in the woods, sitting across from each other. I remember all the ways he taught me to lie. He spent those nights questioning me, asking me where I was from, where I was born, who I was. I am Abdolorean, I answered each time he asked. If I hesitated, even for a moment, we'd begin again. He taught me how to calm my pulse, calm my brain. He taught me to believe in what I said. I pushed down everything I knew about myself, everything I knew to be true. I learned to pretend that I never had other parents, that I wasn't born on Earth.

Who are you? he would ask, and I would tell him what he wanted to hear. *I am Abdolorean,* I said to him, over and over, pushing the truth down to a place I couldn't reach, until my lies became a new kind of truth, or something close enough.

"Officer Li," Chief Hael says, and I look up at him, not used to my new title.

I am Abdolorean, I think, the words pulsing in my veins.

"I'm going to ask you some questions, and I want you to answer them as honestly as you can," he says. "Do you think you can do that for me?"

"Yes, sir," I say, every muscle in my body tense, my brain buzzing with fear.

"Where were you the night Braxon died?" he asks.

"I was at the gala with the rest of the cadets," I answer.

Hael's gaze is cold, assessing, like he knows there's a

lie buried beneath my words and he's trying to figure out just what it is.

"Did you leave the gala at any point in the night?"

"No," I say, shaking my head, fighting the urge to turn to Zo. "I was there the whole time."

"What was the nature of your relationship with Cadet Braxon?" Chief Hael asks, leaning back in his chair and crossing his arms over his chest. "Would you consider him a friend, someone you spent a lot of time with?"

"We were in the same unit during Assessment," I respond, my voice sounding calmer than I feel. "And I'm guessing you already know that he and Zo were together."

Hael's gaze flicks briefly to Zo in the other room and then back to me. "I am aware," he says. "But tell me more about you and Braxon. Your magister informed us that you and he were paired together during one of your practice simulations."

"We were," I allow. I think back to the dark water we moved through, the angry rush of words between us.

Hael stands up from his chair, walking around the table toward me.

"Your magister also stated that Braxon was visibly upset after the simulation," Hael continues. "Would you agree?"

"Yes," I say, my mouth going dry. "He was disappointed, as was I."

Chief Hael leans against the table, and I'm suddenly nervous that he can feel my heart beating.

"Did your relationship with Braxon extend personally outside of the unit?"

"Not really," I say, but I can't help it, I look away from him, to Zo. Her eyes catch mine, and I know I've made a misstep.

"Explain," he says.

I swallow and look back at him. *I am Abdolorean,* I think.

"We were friends with the same people," I tell him. "We spent time together outside of training, but I wouldn't say we were close."

Hael stares at me, watching me in a way I don't know how to read. He turns to Zo.

"You were Braxon's girlfriend," he says.

"Not really," Zo says, her voice bitter. She's still wearing the clothes she slept in. "We were together for a while, but we broke up right before the gala." She pauses, and Chief Hael motions for her to keep talking.

"I caught him with someone else." She crosses her arms over her chest. "With Akia. That was the last time I saw him."

She looks so vulnerable. I wish I could reach out and hold her.

"Where were you for the rest of the night?" he asks.

"I was here," Zo says, shrugging. "I have no idea what Braxon did after I left his place."

Hael looks from Zo to me. It takes all my strength not to think of that night, Braxon's hands clenched around my neck, Braxon collapsing against me.

"What about you, Li? What did you do after the gala ended? Did you go straight home, or did you maybe stop somewhere first?"

He knows. He has to. I open my mouth, about to tell another lie, but Zo cuts me off before I can say anything.

"Li was home by midnight," she tells him. "We played a round of Sudden Death Turbo Ball, this game we made up when we were kids."

She points to the rackets in the corner of the living room, leaning up against the wall. Hael looks at the rackets; then he looks at Zo, at me. I nod. "It's pretty fun, actually," I say, forcing myself to smile.

I can't tell if he believes her, if he believes me. I don't know what he's thinking at all. "We talked about the gala, about what everyone was wearing, then we went to bed," Zo goes on. "We slept in Li's room. We were together all night. And when we woke up the next morning, Braxon's parents beamed me and that's how we found out he was missing."

His gaze lingers on me for a moment too long. "Thank you, both of you, for your time," he says quietly. "If there's anything you hear, anything else you remember from that night, please get in touch."

He heads to the door, walking across the cliff, away from our house, out to the street. I hold my breath until I'm sure he's gone.

Zo comes into the kitchen and sits down with me at the table.

"Why did you say all that?" I ask, my hands trembling. "Why did you tell him I got home before midnight? Why did you—"

"Ryn came by that night," she whispers. "You said you were with him, but I knew he was looking for you. I didn't know why you lied about where you were, but now . . ."

My father comes out from his study, placing his hand on my back, and the truth comes pouring out.

"It was me," I whisper, glancing down at my hands, locked tightly underneath the table. "I killed Braxon."

Zo gasps. I look up at her, pleading. A look of shock flashes across her face.

"I had no choice," I say, my voice wavering. "He figured out who I am. *What* I am." I can't bring myself to tell them that it was my fault—that if I hadn't told Mirabae the truth, Braxon would still be here.

"He attacked me. He tried to kill me. I fought back, but I didn't mean to—"

My words cut off as I start to cry, tears streaming down my face. I pull in a desperate, shaky breath, staring at my family.

"I'm sorry," I whisper.

Zo reaches across the table and takes my hand.

"It's okay," she says quietly. "Nothing on this planet is more important to me than you."

My love for her expands infinitely. I don't know how she could be so selfless, always putting my life before her own.

"You lied for me," I say, and even though she's my sister, even though this is what we always feared and endlessly planned for, it still takes me aback that she did it.

"I've been lying for you my whole life," Zo says softly.

My dad has been standing mutely behind me. He puts his hand against my back, moving it in slow circles.

I'll never be able to express to Zo how grateful I am. I put my hand on her leg. "Are you okay, after all that?" I ask.

"Are you?" she asks, and I don't answer.

Instead, I feel myself break apart, and I start to cry again.

"We'll figure it out, Li, like we always do," my father says, kneeling down in front of me. "Once you get to Penthna, everything will be okay."

"No, Dad," I say, my voice a whisper. "It's not okay. It's never going to be okay. It's only a matter of time. Sooner or later the Agency is going to figure out I killed Braxon, or discover who I am." I take a gasping breath and admit what I knew the moment Hael showed up on our doorstep. "I need to leave the Bay. I need to run."

Zo exchanges a worried look with our father.

"Where would you even go?" she asks, her hand tightening around mine.

"I don't know," I say, my voice shaking. "But I can't go to Penthna, and I can't stay here."

My father presses his palms against his forehead, like he's trying to decide what to do next.

"I'm right, Dad," I say. "You know I'm right. Running away is the safest thing I can do, for myself and for both of you."

For a moment, he's silent; then he takes a breath. He motions for us to sit on the couch. "What I'm about to tell you is something no one else knows," he says, his voice hushed as Zo and I sit down on either side of him.

"Sixteen years ago, just after you were born, Li, I was able to transport a small number of humans out of the Bay, to a colony in the north."

The corners of the room blur together. The floor heaves up beneath me. Everything he says sounds foreign and far away.

"They live along the plains, completely cut off from the rest of the world."

He looks out over the ocean, at the way the water moves.

"What are you saying?" I whisper.

He turns to me and smiles, but his eyes are tinged with sadness.

"I'm saying that you're not the only one left, my love."

His words echo through my head. I'm not the only one left. I'm not the last.

"For the first few years of the colony's existence, everything was too unstable, the danger of discovery too high," he says. "The Agency was ruthless. They were out for blood. There was always the chance the colony would be found and destroyed."

His words fall over me. I let them sink down to a place where they mean something I can understand.

"I promised your parents I would keep you safe," he says quietly. "I'm sorry I didn't tell you sooner. Your life was too precious to risk."

He stands up and paces around the perimeter of the room.

"It will take you one month to reach the north," he says. "Travel along the coast until you get to the border. Don't talk to anyone, don't tell anyone who you are or where you're going. Once you get north, you'll be safe."

"What about you and Zo?" I choke out. "What will happen when I don't show up for my new assignment in the Forces?"

My father shakes his head. "That's not your concern, Li. I'll handle it. Zo and I will be fine."

He turns abruptly and walks into his study. A moment later, he comes back with a pack in his hands.

"Everything you need is in here," he says. "You'll leave tonight."

I look over at Zo. Her breathing is shallow and her eyes brim with tears. She shakes her head wildly, as though she can push everything he's said away.

"Don't go," she whispers. "Li, please, don't go."

I stand up and walk over to her. Wrapping my arms around her shoulders, I hold her as she cries. We both know I'm already gone.

twenty-three

That night, just after the sun sets, I change into pants and a long-sleeved shirt, both made with thread that adjusts to the temperature. Everything I wear is green, like the leaves on the trees in the forest. I think back to the mornings I spent there with my father, so painful at the time, now something I understand. He knew that one day, he would have to let me go. He needed to know that I could survive.

I walk downstairs. My father and sister stand by the door. I pull on my boots, and my father holds the pack out to me, helping me put it onto my shoulders. Zo hands me a piece of paper, folded in half.

"Wait to open it, okay?" she says, her hands shaking.

I wrap my arms around her and hold her tight.

"I love you, Zo," I whisper.

My father presses his hand to the door and it slides open, revealing the earth around us, the ocean below.

"We are always with you." He kisses my forehead. "You're ready, Li," he says.

I can't find the words to say goodbye. The three of us hug; then I break away.

I push myself forward, walking out to the cliff, away from my family, my home. I look back, just once, and I see Zo place her hand over her heart.

There's no moon this far into the forest, no stars, no light at all. I know this land from memory, every shift in the terrain, the roots of every tree. I know exactly where to turn. How many times have I run through the forest, I think numbly, only to be here now, running for my life? My father was always with me then, the danger speculative. I've spent my life planning for a moment like this, and still it doesn't feel real.

I pause to catch my breath, reaching into my pocket for the paper Zo gave me. I open it and see my own face. It's the picture she drew of me so many months ago. The face on the page is my face, but that girl is someone I no longer know, the distance between us unreachable now. I study the picture, tracing its lines with my fingers. So much has changed since that night, back when I was safe, when I thought I knew the shape my life would take.

I know I should just disappear, but I don't know how to leave forever without saying goodbye to Ryn. I run until I reach his street, walking through the garden to the back of the house, where his room is. I pick up a handful of pebbles and toss them at his window. The lights in his room turn on. Ryn appears, pressing his hand to the glass. The window slides open. He leans out and looks down at me.

"Go to the door," he calls out. "I'll let you in."

I walk to the front of his house and wait for him to come downstairs. Ryn opens the door and stands in front of me, shirtless, his hair wild from sleep.

"Ryn," I say, "we need to talk, but not here." We go upstairs, into his room. He closes the door and sits on the bed.

"Li," he says, unnerved. "What is it? What's wrong?"

I sit beside him, trying to find the words I need. I have to tell him everything. I have to tell him what I've done. This, right here, is when it all crashes around me. This is where it ends.

"Ryn," I say, his name catching in my throat. "I'm the one. I killed Braxon."

He stares at me, his face still. I wait for his expression to shift to disbelief, to horror. Instead, he takes my hands in his own.

"He attacked me," I go on. "After the gala. He heard what Mir said; he knew I'm human."

My body shakes as though I'm back there, on the cliffs.

"He was going to kill me. I didn't have any way out."

Ryn nods, asking for no more explanation than the one I've given.

"It's okay, Li," he says, smoothing my hair back. "Everything's going to be okay."

I press my hands up to my face, trying to hold back tears.

I lift my eyes to his and wait for him to say something, anything at all. "I'm just as violent as Abdoloreans believe."

"You did what you had to do to survive," he says. "You're strong and brave, and there's no one I want to be with more, in this galaxy or the next."

I pull him toward me, pressing my lips against his. I kiss him as though it can stop time, as though it can save me. I want to stay in his arms forever, but I know I need to start moving. I pull away and look at him, at the quiet in his eyes.

"I'm running away, Ryn," I say. "I'm not going to Penthna. I'm leaving here, now."

I take a breath and tell him about the north, about the other humans alive on Earth. I tell him that I have to go, that it's the only thing that will protect the people I love. I reach for his hands, searching for some way to say goodbye. He looks at me like he knows what I'm going to say next.

"I'm coming with you," he says.

"You can't leave your life behind," I say. "Not like this. What about your placement? What about Ursna?"

"My life isn't on some other planet. It's on this planet, with you," he says. "No matter what that means. Wherever you go, I'm going. You don't have to do this alone."

"We can never come back to the Bay," I say. I could list all the dangers we'll face, all the risks we'll be taking, but I can tell by the determination in his eyes that there's no way to convince him to stay behind. "We'll never see our families again."

"I know," he says.

He stands up and moves around the room, pulling clothes from his closet, putting his boots on. He's dressed in black, so he'll blend into the forest, into the darkness around us. He shoves supplies into a pack—a knife, hydration capsules, small tools, a fire starter. We walk downstairs and step out into the street. Ryn reaches his hand out to me.

"Are you ready?" he asks.

"Yes," I say.

We walk along the coast for days. All we see is water. All that exists is sand and sky. We collect whatever food we can find, picking beach plums off the bushes that grow low to the ground. We drink from clear streams. We ration the food from our packs. We study the map my father gave me, taking shelter in the caves that run along the shore. We walk as though we know where we're going, like we know what this strange future of ours will hold. We don't speak much, and we don't look behind us. The only sounds are the waves, the wind, our breath.

There are nights when I can't sleep, when I'm woken up by nightmares. On these nights, Ryn sits beside me, drawing designs in the sand with the tips of his fingers. He doesn't ask me what I see in my dreams. We sit together until the sun rises; then we start walking again.

The night before we leave the Bay, Ryn and I lie awake, looking up at the stars.

"Tell me something good," I say.

He wraps his arms around me and talks quietly in the dark.

"Sharks swim while they sleep," he says. "Fish have a two-chambered heart."

He kisses me then, and his lips taste like salt, like the ocean we bathe in.

We wake up before the sun rises. We turn on the transmitter my father put in the pack, listening for the sound of our names, hearing nothing at all. We walk along the edge of the water. The waves wash over our tracks in the sand. We climb up the last cliff on the coast, the one dividing the Bay from the rest of Earth. I turn around and look out at the water. "Goodbye."

The air along the plains is colder than anything we've known before. Most days we go hungry. We get used to this. We get used to lots of things, like walking for days at a time, the silence that settles between us. Each night, Ryn builds a fire. I collect handfuls of grass, whatever branches I can find. Ryn digs a hole in the ground and puts the fire starter between his fingers, a small, flat circle. He snaps and the flames burst to life. We watch the fire burn, and I search for comfort in its small, sacred heat.

"What if we can't find it?" I ask, my voice quiet.

"We'll find it," he says, and the clouds move quickly across the sky.

The days bleed together, one week blurring into the next. Each mile we travel brings us closer to safety. Each day the grief I carry hardens a little more inside me, until it feels like something else, something close to hope.

One morning as we're walking, I look up to see a bird fly across the sky. We stop and watch it, its wings spread wide. The bird carries a branch in its beak.

"Li," says Ryn, studying the map. "We're almost there."

I glance over at him. He's here with me, something real, something I can hold on to. I look up again at the sky stretching over us, the bird far away from us now. We take off across the plains and the land spreads out before us, shining with the light of the sun.

Go, my heart beats. *Go.*

acknowledgments

Thank you first to my family. To my mother, for raising me right, for standing behind me in everything. To my father, for always believing that writing was something I could do. To Seth Blogier, best brother, who continues to amaze me with his creative vision. To the rest of my family, the whole mess of you, your love lifts me up.

Thank you to Josh Bank, for taking this idea and running with it. Thank you to Annie Stone, for guiding me through the beginning of this book. Thank you to Eliza Swift, for leading this story toward its true north. Thank you to Sara Shandler, for her incredible dedication to and insights into this story. Thank you to Wendy Loggia, for being an amazing editor, and for giving this book a home.

Thank you to Mallory Grigg, for creating a beautiful cover that captures the universe. To everyone at Alloy and Random House who worked to bring this book to life, thank you so very much. To Hannah Pepper-Cunningham and Rachel Cole, my oldest and dearest, for their deep and unending friendship, for continually inspiring me with the art they make. To Kendell Newman, for her writerly support all the way from the tundra. To Yoko Feinman, for her eyes and her soul, for her heart. To Billy Gildea, for everything, for it all.